LION BY THE LAKE

'So there should be no lions at all left in this area?' Adam Hope said.

Levina nodded. 'That's right.'

'So it's possible that the wardens left one behind?' Emily Hope glanced with concern at Mandy.

Levina sighed. 'If Mandy and James are right about what they saw this morning.'

Mandy's heart sank lower than ever. She wished she could say no, they'd been mistaken; the lion-cub hadn't been all alone and calling for its mother. She would have given anything at that moment to have been proved wrong.

But Joseph confirmed what they had seen. 'Lion-cub calling across the lake. No mother.'

LUCY DANIELS

Lion
— *by the* —
Lake

Illustrations by Jenny Gregory

*Hodder
Children's
Books*

a division of Hodder Headline plc

For all the wonderful people we met in Africa

Special thanks to Jenny Oldfield
**Thanks also to C. J. Hall, B.Vet.Med., M.R.C.V.S., for reviewing
the veterinary material contained in this book.**

Text copyright © 1997 Ben M. Baglio
Created by Ben M. Baglio, London W6 0HE
Illustrations copyright © 1997 Jenny Gregory
Cover art copyright © 1997 Peter Warner

First published in Great Britain in 1997
by Hodder Children's Books

A Catalogue record for this book is available from the British Library

ISBN 0 340 68718 5

Typeset by Avon Dataset Ltd, Bidford-on-Avon, Warks

Printed and bound in Great Britain by
Clays Ltd, St Ives plc

Hodder Children's Books
a division of Hodder Headline plc
338 Euston Road
London NW1 3BH

One

'Over there, by the water!' James whispered and pointed.

Mandy Hope couldn't believe her luck. It was her first day in Africa, the start of a long summer safari with her family, and her friend James Hunter. And now James was telling her that the very animal she most longed to see – king of the beasts, a lion – was just ahead of them!

'Where?' Mandy peered into the tall grass by the lakeside.

'In the shade of that big red rock. Shh, he's standing up! I think he's spotted us!'

She heard a rustling sound in the dry yellow

grass. There was a movement. But still she couldn't see the lion. Perhaps James was mistaken. Mandy stood on tiptoe and leaned out of the open-topped jeep.

She saw the rustling grass and the rock. Thorntree branches fanned out above it to give shade from the high sun. And beyond the tree she could see what seemed like miles of shimmering blue water and the misty mountains rising from the far shore of Lake Kasanka.

'I can't see him!' Mandy screwed up her eyes and leaned further out.

Joseph, their driver, sat at the wheel and peered through the windscreen. His expert senses recognised every movement, every sound of lion in the bush.

'Now I've lost him, too. I think he's gone.' James sounded suddenly flat. He glanced down at Joseph.

The driver shook his head. 'Small one,' he said in his rumbling voice. 'Alone.'

A lion-cub then? And by himself? Mandy stared intently at every blade of grass, every moving shadow.

Joseph was the first to see the cub when it reappeared. 'There.' He pointed.

And now Mandy could hear a soft growling.

She followed the direction of the sound. It came from beyond the rock, from a stretch of pebbly red sand that led to the water's edge. Then at last she saw it. The cub crept across the sand to the lake. It stood, head raised, ears pricked, growling across the vast stretch of water.

It was the first lion Mandy had ever seen living in the wild. She felt her heart leap and she clutched the roof of the jeep. She blinked and opened her eyes, half expecting the cub to be gone. This wasn't real; Africa, the lake, the Ruwenzori Mountains, they were all a dream. But no, the cub stood and called out, his young, rough coat covered in beautiful brown markings, his long tail swishing. He pricked his round ears and listened for an answer to his call.

'How old is he?' James whispered.

'Six months, maybe less,' Joseph said. 'Not old enough to be alone.'

'Why is he growling?' Mandy asked.

The cub ignored their jeep and strode off along the sand. His large paws made perfect prints as he went.

'He's calling his mother.'

'She can't be far away, can she?' Mandy knew that lionesses took good care of their young.

This time Joseph made no reply.

They watched eagerly as the cub turned tail and trotted rapidly towards them. His chest was pure white, his eyes big and golden. He came close to their jeep, looked up and whimpered.

'He must be lost.' James voiced their fear.

'But he'll be OK, he can look after himself.' Mandy scanned the pebbly shore, the tall grass and the bushes. The cub was roughly the size of a Border collie back home in Yorkshire. 'He's big and strong, he can fight off enemies,' she said. She watched him rear up on his hind legs and rest his huge front paws against the door of their jeep. He gazed straight into her eyes. 'You're beautiful,' she breathed. 'And you're not scared of us, are you?'

Again, Joseph said nothing. He wanted to see what the cub would do next.

The young lion inspected the jeep, still growling softly. Then he dropped to the ground. Mandy heard James let out a deeply-held breath. She stared down at the cub as he began to pad away towards the spiky bushes. Whatever he was looking for, he hadn't found it here.

'Don't go!' Mandy pleaded. For her the lion was a magical creature. She watched sadly as he slipped from sight.

Minutes passed. The sun rose higher. By now

the morning breeze from the mountains had dropped and the earth began to bake in the sun's heat. Mandy stared at the spot where the cub had vanished.

'He's not coming back,' James said at last.

From the driver's seat Joseph nodded once. 'Ready?' he asked. He started the engine.

Mandy sighed and slid down into the jeep. 'I can't believe he actually came so close! He was this far away!' She spread her arms to show the distance. 'If I'd wanted to, I could have reached out and touched him!'

'It's a good job you didn't. He might not have liked it,' James reminded her.

They clung on as the jeep set off and lurched across the rough ground. Joseph headed back to camp. As they jolted away from the lake, strange, bright blue birds rose from the bush and flew off, while small, quick foxes and fat warthogs broke cover and ran ahead of them.

Close to Kampi ya Simba, the jeep slowed down within walking distance of the long, low wooden hut and the tents that surrounded it. A party of baboons swung down from a huge baobab tree. They surrounded the car, poked their long, black faces through the windows, then ran off chattering in all directions.

Joseph pulled on the handbrake and nodded. It was safe now to run across the dirt yard and on to the veranda. So Mandy and James tumbled out of the jeep and headed for the hut, breathless with excitement. They ran into the research station to find Mandy's mum and dad.

'We've seen a lion!' Mandy cried as she leaped up the single wooden step, across the veranda and into the office. 'James spotted him first. It was great. He was a young cub . . . this big! We watched him for ages. He came right up to us. He was absolutely gorgeous!'

Adam and Emily Hope had brought Mandy and James to Africa on a working holiday. They had left their practice in Welford, Yorkshire, in the safe hands of Simon, their nurse, and a stand-in vet, Alistair King, who had travelled all the way from Australia to help out. They knew that the patients at Animal Ark would get the very best care while they were away.

It had been Mandy's mum's idea. 'We need a break!' she'd announced, one night in January that year. The days were cold and short, the nights long, and it was a very busy time. Dogs and cats, like people, got sick in the winter with colds and flu, farm animals didn't like the frost, and then there was the never-ending round of vaccinations to be done and minor ailments to be cured. 'I feel worn out,' she'd confessed.

'Africa!' Adam Hope had come out with it just like that. 'We can visit Levina at Lake Kasanka. She's always inviting us out to see her.'

Dr Levina Lemiso was a friend from the Hopes' time at veterinary college in York. Born in Tanzania, she had come to England to study. She'd loved living in Yorkshire, but her heart was in Africa. Now she was back in her homeland working as a research scientist in the Ruwenzori Crater.

Mandy's eyes had lit up. 'When?' She pictured the animals she might see. 'Will there be rhinos and hippos? And giraffes and elephants? And *lions*?' These, above all, were the animals she loved to watch on the wildlife programmes on television. 'When can we go?'

'This summer.' Adam Hope had made up his mind. 'We can learn a lot from Levina, and you can bring James along if you like. He'll like it out there, too.'

They'd asked Mr and Mrs Hunter's permission, then spent the rest of the winter and spring planning their trip. Levina had been overjoyed at the news; now she could return her friends' kindness, she said. They could fly out and join her at Kampi ya Simba, the Camp of the Lions, and she would show them her work with the animals of the volcanic crater. Mandy and James began to tick off each day on the calendar until the day in July when they were due to depart.

Then they'd said a sad goodbye to Animal Ark and all their friends; goodbye to Gran and Grandad Hope, to Simon, and to Jean who worked in Reception. They'd handed over to Alistair, and, as their plane flew over Mount Kilimanjaro and its snowy summit broke through the clouds, they'd said hello to Africa and to a new, summer-long adventure.

Now Adam Hope sat back in his chair as Mandy and James burst into Levina's office. 'Where's the fire?' he joked. It seemed that Mandy had enjoyed her first morning by the lake. Words tumbled out as she flung her dusty baseball cap on to the table.

'You should have seen him, Dad! He came right up to us, and he was so cute. He was covered in dark brown spots, like a furry leopard . . .' Mandy couldn't get over her encounter with the king of African animals.

'Rosettes,' her father said, smiling. 'The markings are called rosettes. They fade when the cub is about ten months old.'

'Whatever. I've never seen anything so adorable, honestly! He had big yellow eyes and a sweet little black nose, and big, big paws . . . !'

Emily Hope came in from a side room. She had wound her long red hair into a bun to keep cool in the heat, and wore a sleeveless white T-shirt and shorts. Her face had already freckled in the sun. 'What are we talking about?' she quizzed James, who stood to one side as Mandy chattered on.

'A lion-cub.' He tipped the peak of his own cap back from his forehead. 'It was only about six months old, we think.'

'With his mother?' Mrs Hope wanted to know more. She smiled at Joseph as he followed James and Mandy into the office.

'*Jambo*.' The old driver hovered by the door. He gave a Swahili greeting, a language used by all the tribes in this part of Africa.

'*Jambo*, Joseph. I hear you drove out and found a lion-cub?'

'By the lake.' Instead of smiling back, Joseph gave a slight frown.

'Is there something wrong?'

He shrugged. 'There was no mother, no brothers, no sisters.'

'And should there have been?' Emily Hope asked.

Mandy stopped talking and tuned in to her mother's question. 'We guess his family must have been nearby but well-hidden. He wouldn't wander far by himself, would he?' She too turned to Joseph for an answer.

But before the old man could explain his worries, Levina herself came quietly into the room. She listened thoughtfully to the end of Mandy's query. 'Not normally,' she broke in. 'But this is not a normal time for the lions of Lake Kasanka.'

Mandy turned towards the small, slight figure dressed in bright yellow and red. Levina wore the costume of her people; a length of printed cotton wound round her hips and worn as a long skirt, another wrapped tightly round her chest. From their first sight of her at the airport the day before, Mandy had warmed to this calm and friendly woman.

'Why, what's happened?' Adam Hope sounded puzzled. 'I thought the whole crater area was good lion country? There's plenty of cover amongst the rocks and trees, and certainly plenty of deer for them to hunt.' Great herds of graceful impala roamed the flat valley floor, formed when an long-extinct volcano had erupted and then died.

'Normally, yes,' Levina said again. She went out on to the veranda and waited for the others to follow.

'Let me explain. From here at Kampi ya Simba you can see the whole of the crater. There is the lake, and there in the distance are the Mountains of the Moon.'

'Is that what *Ruwenzori* means?' James asked.

Levina nodded. 'There, where the mountains meet the water, is protected land. We call it the Ruwenzori National Park. There all the animals live safe from hunters, poachers and suchlike.' She told the story in a low, soft voice. 'But here on the southern side of the lake there is no national park and no safety for the rhino and the leopard, the mighty elephant and the lion. Here hunters may hunt and farmers may kill the animals who prey on their cattle.'

Mandy took a sharp breath and glanced at James. He had screwed up his eyes tight behind his glasses which glinted in the sun. He peered at the distant mountains.

'That's why we have this research station here on the southern side of the lake. We have another by the lakeside, and others on the

Lion by the lake

northern shore. Our job is to tag as many of the animals as possible with radio transmitters and trace their movements across the crater. It also means we can keep count of how many lions and other big cats are killed.'

Mandy felt the word 'killed' drop like a stone into the conversation.

'Who kills them?' Adam Hope spoke urgently. He strode out into the yard, as if ready to put a stop to it then and there.

'Not poachers, as you might think,' Levina explained patiently. 'No, it's mostly the cattle herders in the west.' She pointed to a flat plain where the sun had begun to cast longer shadows. It stretched to the western rim of the crater, too far to see the herds of cattle which Levina described. 'They blame the lions for attacking their herds, then they apply to the government for a permit to shoot them.'

'How can they do that?' Mandy's blood ran cold as she appealed to Joseph. Africa suddenly seemed a dangerous place for the beautiful cub they'd seen trotting gracefully by the water's edge.

The old man stopped in the doorway, hat in hand. He shrugged and let Levina continue.

'They have their reasons. In any case, two

lions have been shot dead this month alone. It became time for us to act, so we called in the park wardens from across the lake. They agreed to round up the three prides of lions who had marked out their territory on this southern shore. The plan was to tranquillise them and shift them in crates up to the park where they would be safe. It was a difficult job and they've only just completed it.' Levina finished her story and turned to Adam Hope.

'So, what you mean to say is that there should be no lions at all left in this area?' Adam Hope said.

She nodded. 'That's right. We know for sure that the wardens rounded up all the adult lions because they're the ones we managed to tag in the past. In total there were three males and fifteen females. But we don't tag the young ones until they're weaned and ready to leave the mother.'

'So it's possible that the wardens left one behind?' Emily Hope was the first to realise exactly what might have happened. She glanced with concern at Mandy.

After a long pause Levina sighed and nodded. 'If Mandy and James are right about what they saw this morning.'

Mandy's heart sank lower than ever. She wished she could say no, they had been mistaken; the lion-cub hadn't been where they said it was, all alone and calling for its mother. She would have given anything at that moment to have been proved wrong.

But Joseph confirmed what they had seen. 'Lion-cub calling across the lake. No mother.'

Mandy stared at James, then out across the bush towards the silver-blue lake. It was a magnificent sight, so different from what she'd always known back home in green and pleasant Welford.

Here the sun baked the land until the heat shimmered off it in a wobbly haze. The sky was so blue it looked unreal. She loved the strangeness, could hardly wait to go out and explore once more. But there was fear mixed in with her excitement, for out there somewhere, hidden in the tall grass or roaming westwards towards the cattle herds in search of much-needed food, was their hungry lion-cub, alone and in danger.

Two

That night, Mandy lay awake for a long time. The visitors were sleeping outside the research station in small, one-man tents, and she could hear the whoops and cries of strange animals, sometimes faint and faraway, sometimes so close that she would switch on her torch to see if by any chance some small creature had broken in. But the white domed tent was empty except for her and her waking dreams and fears.

'Mandy, are you asleep?'

She heard James's voice call softly from the next tent. It was past midnight. The grown-ups were sleeping soundly in their tents after a supper stewed slowly over an open fire by Thomas, the camp cook. 'No,' she answered. 'What's wrong? Can't you get to sleep either?'

'No. I can't stop thinking about that poor cub.'

'Me neither.' She sighed, then let a silence grow in the darkness before she confessed what it was that was keeping her awake. 'I asked Levina what would happen to him now.'

'What did she say?'

'At first she just shook her head. But I said I wanted to know, even if it was bad.'

'And is it?' James whispered.

'Not all of it.' Mandy decided to unzip her tent so that she could look out at the stars while they talked. She heard James do the same. 'For a start, she said that the cub is probably fully weaned, which means he doesn't need his mother's milk any more. And he'll have been eating solid food since he was about two months old, so that's no problem either.'

'But?' James peered out of his tent, his face pale in the moonlight, his dark fringe hanging over his forehead.

'But he won't have learned how to hunt properly yet. He'll still rely on his mother to kill the prey and bring the meat to him.'

'So he must be pretty hungry by now. When

did the wardens take the other lions up to Ruwenzori?'

'Levina says it was two days ago.' Mandy jumped as a night-time creature howled in the bushes behind the hut.

'There's something else, isn't there?' James waited for the rest of the bad news.

'She says that the cub will probably be in danger from other animals like hyenas and jackals. That's why lions normally stick together. Young ones should stay with the pride until they're at least eighteen months old.'

James gave himself time to let the information sink in. 'And what did Levina say about the farmers who want to hunt the lions?'

Mandy sighed. 'I don't know. I didn't ask. It was already bad enough, without thinking of men and their guns.'

There was a long, deep silence.

'Maybe they'll think that all the lions have gone from round here,' James suggested. 'They're not to know that the wardens made a mistake and left one behind.'

Mandy stared up at the stars. The Milky Way spread like a long stream of glittering mist across the sky. 'Let's hope so,' she whispered.

They'd run out of things to say, but neither

felt like sleep. They each held a clear picture of the cub in their memories; his eyes shining golden like the sun. He'd seemed to look up at them and ask for their help.

'I've had an idea!' James's voice came out of the darkness after what seemed like an age.

Mandy turned to listen.

'Levina has a small radio transmitter in the office, doesn't she?'

She nodded. 'She needs it to keep in contact with the other scientists in the crater.'

'Yes, and they pick up signals on it from the animals they've tagged. That means we can make contact with the wardens in the national park!'

Mandy thought for a while. 'Instead of by phone, you mean?' She knew there were no telephone links this far out in the bush. 'Then what?' Slowly she began to see what James was getting at.

'Then we can ask them to come back here and collect the cub,' he said, more loudly than he'd intended. There was a yelp from a nearby bush as a startled animal skittered off.

'And they can take him to the park to find the rest of his pride! Brilliant!' Mandy could always rely on James to think clearly and come up with an answer. Sometimes her own head got too clouded with worry about animals who might be suffering. 'Oh, James, that's a great idea. Let's ask Levina first thing in the morning!'

It seemed so simple. They smiled and nodded. Mandy sighed with relief.

James was pleased with himself as he thought aloud. 'See, it'll be the wardens' job to get the cub back together with his mother, and then no one will be allowed to hunt him in the park, will they?'

Soon they agreed to zip up their tents and try to sleep.

'Morning will come quicker if we do,' James told her.

Zip-zip . . . Zip-zip! This was the sound of James and Mandy trying to be sensible, being patient. But their thoughts still whirled inside their heads. They pictured the wardens speeding down in their jeep as soon as it grew light. Perhaps James and Mandy would even be allowed to help rescue the cub, and then go to watch him being released to rejoin his worried family?

Mandy charged on in her imagination, and when she did finally fall asleep in the dead of night, she dreamed of lions blinking in the sunlight and of lionesses grooming their cubs with their rough, pink tongues.

Thomas was up at dawn to cook a breakfast of eggs, bread and tea. A cold mist had rolled down the mountainside into the crater. He worked quietly to light the fire and boil the water.

Mandy opened her eyes to the rattle of pans and metal cups. So she'd slept after all? She hadn't really seen their cub meeting up with his mother and the rest of his pride? No, that was still to come!

She scrambled out of her warm sleeping bag and into her T-shirt and shorts. Quickly she tied her blonde hair back, then she crawled out and hurried towards the smoking fire.

James made it at the same time, his hair tousled, his face pink and freckled from yesterday's sun. 'It's cold!' he shivered. 'Who would believe it? We're in the middle of Africa and it's freezing!'

Thomas grinned shyly as he carried a large pan of steaming water on to the veranda. He began to make the tea. Not much older than Mandy and James, his actions were quick and skilled. He soon came back and stirred the eggs.

By this time another tent was being unzipped.

Emily Hope emerged on hands and knees, warmly dressed in her green fleece-jacket. She stood and gazed at the mountains shrouded in mist, took a deep breath and smiled at Mandy and James.

'*Tee-ea*!' a voice moaned feebly from inside the tent. It was Mandy's dad.

'It's ready; come out and get it!' Mandy cried. 'You'll miss the sunrise if you don't get up soon!'

'Good!' Adam Hope groaned. 'What time do you call this? I thought I was supposed to be on holiday!'

Emily Hope winked at Mandy. 'You are, but you can't miss this brilliant sunrise!' she called.

Grumbling, he poked his head out of the tent. He rubbed his eyes and looked blearily at the busy scene. 'What does a person have to do round here to get a cup of tea?'

'Dad, you look as if you've been trampled by an elephant!' Mandy laughed. His beard was rumpled, his brown hair sticking up, and his blue T-shirt looked as if he hadn't taken it off for days.

'I feel as if I have.' He creaked and groaned as he stood up.

At last Mandy softened and took him his mug of tea. 'Dad, we've been thinking . . .' she began.

'Oh no, it's too early in the morning for that!' he protested.

'No, really. James thought of it. We have to ask Levina first, but it's a great idea.'

'What is?' Levina herself emerged from the office. She was already up and dressed in an orange and green robe with a matching turban wound round her head.

James spotted her and ran up to join Mandy. 'We've thought of how we can rescue the cub!' he said eagerly.

'Have you, now?' Levina raised her eyebrows.

Emily Hope smiled at her. 'Don't worry, Levina; once you get to know these two, you'll realise that if there's an animal round here who needs rescuing, they'll do it, come what may!'

Their friend nodded. 'That's good. But this is Africa, remember. To rescue a lion-cub here is not the same as to rescue a little kitten back home. At six months old this cub is big and strong. His claws can hurt.'

Mandy made it clear that she understood. 'We know. That's why we don't plan to do it all by ourselves.'

'Well, that's a relief.' Her dad wandered up, mug in hand. 'Levina's right. These animals are as wild as you can get. It's best to leave things to the experts.'

'Like who, for instance?' Mandy's eyes had begun to twinkle. She sneaked a cheeky look at James.

'Well, like Levina here. Or like the park wardens . . .' Adam Hope saw that Mandy had something up her sleeve.

She grinned. 'Exactly! You tell him, James!'

Blushing, James explained their idea. 'We thought the wardens would want to help once they found out their mistake. And then we thought maybe we could go with them and see the rest of the lions in the mountains.' He hopped from one foot to the other, wondering if it would work out the way they wanted.

'Possibly,' Levina said slowly. She never hurried. 'But I can't promise.'

'Can we try?' Mandy asked eagerly.

'Yes, you can try; after breakfast.'

'Eggs!' Thomas held up a pan and made the announcement. He began to spoon scrambled egg on to the slices of bread.

So Mandy and James had to wait ten whole minutes while everyone ate their food. Ten whole minutes of guessing what the wardens' answer would be, of trying to swallow scrambled egg in their excitement, of hoping and praying that they were still in time to save their lion-cub.

The radio crackled and whined from its shelf in Levina's room. She pressed more buttons to find the right frequency for the warden's office at the Ruwenzori National Park.

'*Jambo*. This is Levina Lemiso. Is that Matthew Mulakesi? This is Levina Lemiso. Can you hear me?'

A woman's voice crackled back over the transmitter. '*Jambo*, Levina. *Habari*? – How are you? – This is Matthew's wife, Joan Mulakesi. Matthew is out. What brings you on the line so early?'

'We need your help, Joan. We have a lion-cub here by the lakeside. Matthew and his team must have left him behind.' Levina smiled confidently at Mandy. 'We'd like to know if they could come back for him.'

'When?' There was another fuzz of noise and static, more whistling and whining.

'As soon as possible. We don't think the cub will last long all by himself.'

There was a pause while the station cleared. 'I'm sorry, Levina. Matthew has taken everyone up north. We heard there were elephant poachers on the border and they went to warn then off.' Joan sounded genuinely sad that her husband wasn't there to help.

Mandy felt her high hopes crash. She listened quietly, still wanting to believe that there was a way round the problem.

'When will they be back?' Levina asked.

'Three or four days. It depends.'

'So long?' Even Levina sounded helpless. She sighed and shook her head. 'OK, thanks, Joan. It was our best chance of saving the cub, but never mind.' Reluctantly she switched off contact with the wardens' office and turned to the others.

'What now?' Emily Hope spoke for them all.

'Now all we can do is go about our own business and hope to come across the cub ourselves.' Levina was practical, but she didn't sound hopeful. 'If we do find him we'll bring him back here and keep him until Matthew shows up.'

'Is that better than letting him stay out in the bush?'

'Yes. At least here we can feed him. If he continues to wander free, sooner or later a hyena will get him. You can be sure of that.'

'But will we have to keep him locked up?' As soon as she'd said it, Mandy hated the idea.

'I'm afraid so. And then of course it also becomes more difficult to release him into the wild.' Levina looked away and began to sift through papers on her desk. She felt everyone's disappointment in the silence that followed.

Adam Hope scratched his forehead. 'You mean, if the cub builds up a lot of contact with us humans, he'll begin to grow too tame?'

'Like a pet?' James added.

'Too tame and too trusting,' Levina agreed. 'And you know, a wild animal should not rely too much on human beings.' She smiled sadly.

Mandy thought frantically. 'But at least he

would still stand a chance if we looked after him!'

The others nodded their agreement.

'So we should try!' she insisted. She couldn't bear the idea of leaving the cub to the mercy of the hyenas.

'Very well.' At last Levina agreed.

They made a plan. As Thomas cleared away the breakfast things, Adam and Emily Hope decided to take one of the jeeps and head west to the plain where the farmers' cattle grazed. Everyone thought there was a fair chance that this was where the cub had gone.

Meanwhile, Mandy and James agreed to go with Joseph to the lakeside, to the place where they had first spotted him.

'You might need this crate,' Levina told them. She handed James a large wooden box with a wire front. He put it in the back of the jeep. 'If you do find the cub, Joseph will help you coax him into the box with scraps of meat from this bag.' She handed Mandy a plastic sack. 'But be careful. Remember what I told you; this cub will be fierce. Keep well clear of his claws and his teeth.'

They nodded. Mandy glanced out at the open plain. Already her mum and dad's jeep was disappearing into the distance in a cloud of red dust. Between them surely they must be able to track down the lion cub.

'Good luck!' Levina waved them off. She and Thomas promised to search the area around the research station.

And so they set off before the sun had gathered its full strength, across the scrubby bushland towards Lake Kasanka. There, ahead of them, Mandy gazed in amazement at the white-fringed shore where Joseph said that salt had formed as the water evaporated. Beyond this was a pink band; thousands of flamingos stood feeding at the water's edge. From here she thought they looked like a pale pink cloud. And on the way to the water they passed the slim brown impala with their long, pointed horns, the heavy wildebeest with their thick necks and big heads. Joseph would point them out and Mandy and James found each and every one of them new and wonderful. But still they longed to see the lion-cub. They kept their eyes peeled and studied the bush.

'Giraffe!' Joseph braked and pointed to the horizon.

Mandy could see three tall shapes loping towards a cluster of thorntrees. They rocked forwards on long legs, ungainly necks dipping and swaying as they ran. The sight took her breath away, but still she didn't want to stop.

'Let's go!' James urged, as anxious as she was.

So the jeep rolled on, until at last they reached the lake.

'I go slow now,' Joseph told them. The engine roar fell to a murmur as the jeep crept along the pebbled shore.

Nearby, some of the flamingos raised their heads and nervously lifted their long red legs out of the water. But they let the jeep pass slowly by.

'No luck,' James sighed. He raised his glasses to rub his tired eyes.

'At least the mist has gone.' Mandy scanned the scene near and far, under trees, beneath rocks. 'We should find him sooner or later!' The sun had risen high in the sky, and the cool morning had quickly turned hot as the jeep crawled on, zig-zagging across the level floor of the crater.

'Hyena!' Joseph warned.

Mandy gripped the side of the jeep. She strained to see. Yes, there in the tall fawn grass was a grey shape, spotted and silent. His head was up, his mouth hung open. The hyena stood, still as stone, watching his hidden prey.

'Here they come!' Joseph pointed again to where three more hunters skirted round the far side of a tall rock, eyes fixed on their victim, creeping up from behind.

Then Mandy and James saw a solitary gazelle raise its head and sniff the air. They held their breaths, desperate for the gazelle to sense danger. Suddenly it did. It leaped away and sprang across the grass to join its herd. The first hyena dropped its head and sloped off on another hunt. Mandy swallowed hard and asked Joseph to drive on in the silent heat.

A couple of hours passed in a haze. They drove by towers of green cacti and the fat grey trunks of baobab trees. Huge orange flowers blossomed on dark green bushes, and the same bright blue birds as yesterday flew up wherever they went.

But still there was no sign of the cub. Even Joseph had to admit that it would soon be time to give up. 'Maybe hyena?' he said with a shrug. Meaning, 'Maybe the hyenas found the cub before we did.'

Mandy shuddered. It had been a long time since they'd seen any movement in the bush. The hot sun had sent most animals to rest in the shade or down to the water to drink. She spotted zebra by the lake, their black and white stripes standing out against the blue water.

'Look at that!' James grabbed her arm. 'Drive, Joseph, quickly!'

Joseph followed James's pointing finger and Mandy saw the zebra herd look up from their drinking. A shiver of alarm seemed to pass through them. One or two skittered out of the water on to the beach.

'Something's wrong,' James said.

They hung on tight as the jeep gathered speed. By now the zebra were definitely frightened by something in the bush. They clustered together, rearing up and jostling this way and that.

'Maybe it's our cub creeping up on them!' Mandy whispered.

'Or another hyena.' James warned her not to get her hopes up too high. 'Let's wait and see.'

Whatever it was, the zebra still shifted nervously. One broke away at the far edge of the herd. Others turned to follow. It seemed that the danger lay behind a thorntree.

'That's the same tree as yesterday!' Mandy gasped. She recognised the rock beneath and the fan-shaped branches. 'This is where we first saw the cub!'

The whole herd had begun to flee. The animals sent up a great cloud of dust. Mandy heard thundering hooves, but she could see nothing. They would have to wait. Joseph stopped the jeep and let the red dust billow round them.

'Please let it be him!' Mandy closed her eyes. The same tree, the same rock as before, the same time of day! There, somewhere, she was sure their hungry lion-cub lay and stalked his prey, just as his mother had shown him.

Soon the dust began to settle. She peered through the thinning cloud. And yes; there *was* a shape appearing. But it was too tall and thin to be their cub. It stood upright; a human figure cloaked in crimson, still and silent.

They waited until at last the dust had cleared. Fear caught at Mandy and clutched at her dry throat. The figure didn't move. It stared at them, eyes gazing steadily, whites luminous against the dark face, the neck hung with heavy beads, red, white and black. The long legs and feet were bare.

'Who's that?' James whispered. They froze under the boy's gaze.

He watched them silently. Only his eyes moved as Joseph got out of the jeep and approached him.

Slowly the driver raised one hand to greet him. '*Jambo!*' he said.

Three

To Mandy, it seemed as if the boy had appeared by magic. One second he was invisible, the next he was standing there. 'Where did he come from?' she said when she found her voice.

'Search me.' James watched quietly as Joseph went to greet the strange figure.

The boy raised his hand in warning. He listened to the zebras' thundering hooves. Then he spoke rapidly to Joseph in Swahili.

'What's he doing here?' Mandy was suspicious. The native boy looked fierce. He didn't smile as he spoke. He jabbed his finger in the direction of the zebra, then turned towards the lake.

'He's probably out hunting,' James guessed. The boy carried a long, pointed stick. 'Maybe he was lying in wait.'

'For our cub?' she gasped. She almost jumped out of the jeep to run and protest, but James held her back. 'Perhaps word got around. Do they hunt lions round here?' Levina hadn't included the local tribes in her list of dangers to the cub, but it seemed possible that they too would want to hunt him down. Her heart raced with a mixture of fear and anger.

'I don't know.' James kept his head. He saw Joseph turn and come back towards them while the boy stepped into the shade of a tree.

'What did he say?' Mandy called. The conversation had been abrupt. Joseph was walking quickly.

'Come here,' he said, beckoning them. He glanced over his shoulder at the boy.

James checked with Mandy. 'I think he wants us to go and talk to him.'

She nodded.

'Come!' Joseph said again, impatient now.

'Do you feel as scared as I do?' Mandy asked. The boy stared at them from the dark shadows, his crimson cloak flung across one shoulder, his neck circled by a wide bead collar. Clasped in his strong fingers, the long staff looked dangerous.

'Yep,' James admitted. He took a quick breath and opened the door of the jeep. 'But I'm not going to let him know it!'

They stepped on to the dusty red earth together.

'Simba,' Joseph said in his rumbling voice. He led the way back to the boy.

'Lion?' James translated. '*Simba* means lion. It sounds as if the boy's seen the cub, at any rate!'

They broke into a run to catch up with Joseph. News, any news, was better than none.

'Where?' Mandy gasped. She looked all around for a sign. Maybe they would see prints in the dust, or perhaps the boy had cornered the cub close by.

'What's going on?' James asked Joseph when they came up beside him.

'Listen.' Joseph didn't answer directly. Instead, he took them closer to the boy. 'He says the cub was nearby. There are fresh prints by the water. The zebra smelled lion in the wind.'

'Is that why they ran off?'

'Yes. But our jeep frightened the cub. Now he's gone again.'

Thank heavens! Mandy thought. *If the boy had got any closer, he might have killed him!* She wondered why Joseph took it so calmly, knowing that their cub was in danger.

'This boy knows the lions of Lake Kasanka,' Joseph told them. 'Come and hear what he has to say.'

'Does he speak English?' James wondered.

'Yes, he learns it at school. He knows where the lions sleep, where they hunt, when they come to the lake to drink. Listen.'

They had reached the shade of the bare, spiky tree where the boy stood. Mandy could feel his strong, silent presence. She held her breath.

He took a step towards them. 'The cub was here by the water. You made much noise. He went.' The boy's voice was slow and soft.

Close to, Mandy saw that his eyes were calm, not fierce. 'Could you find him again?'

He nodded.

'Of course,' Joseph broke in. 'He has a gift, this boy. His name is Simba.'

A faint, proud smile passed over the boy's lips.

James frowned. 'Why do they call him "Lion"?'

'Because of his great friendship with them.

Simba, the lion-boy. That is his name.'

'Friendship?' Mandy echoed. 'You mean he doesn't plan to hunt our cub?'

Joseph chuckled. 'Hunt? No, Simba is the lions' best friend.'

Again the boy smiled and nodded.

'But we must go fast,' the old man reminded them. 'The cub is weak from hunger. He can't hunt, but there are many round here who would hunt him!'

'I get it!' James came in with an excited cry. 'Simba here can help us find the cub and save him!'

Simba held up his head proudly. He was listening, yet not listening, to their talk. He seemed to see and hear the smallest movement in the bush.

'Be quiet,' Joseph warned. 'It's almost noon. Simba says the cub will soon come back to drink.'

'What should we do?' Mandy glanced at the jeep. 'Shall we go and fetch the crate?' She wanted to be ready to capture the cub.

''No. Do as Simba does. Make no noise.'

So they withdrew into the shadow of the tree. The sun was directly overhead, beating down on the blue lake. A heat haze shimmered over the red earth. Nothing moved.

Mandy looked at James. Here they were in a huge landscape, hotter than they'd ever known, a million miles from the rolling hills and rainy summers of Welford. She had to pinch herself to remind herself that she was really here.

Then a single bird flew up from the shore; a large black and white bird with a curved bill. The ibis startled a group of flamingos at the water's edge. Simba stooped and began to creep towards them.

Joseph urged James and Mandy to follow. 'Lion,' he murmured.

They crouched and crept forward. The boy managed to move without a sound, planting his bare feet carefully on the baked earth. He carried his long stick level to the ground. His eyes darted this way and that.

Then he stopped. Mandy and James froze behind him. They followed Simba's gaze towards a clump of dry grass only metres from the water. Mandy heard it rustle. Was it the breeze? Or was it their lion?

The boy warned them silently not to move. He crept on alone.

She saw the flamingos settle and dip their beaks to feed once more. Her own nerves were on edge. Their first sight of Simba had given her a cold shock that still lingered. Could they really trust him not to harm the lion?

In her own mind she got ready to step in and save the cub. If Simba so much as raised the stick against him, she would jump in and stop him. She tensed, ready to act.

Simba looked and listened. He turned his head a fraction. He waited.

At last Mandy could see what he had seen. There, hidden in the brown grass, was a small pair of ears, two yellow eyes, a whiskered face. The animal turned his head sideways to watch Simba. It was their cub!

He lay in the heat, perfectly camouflaged in the grass. Only the twitching of his ears gave him away. Mandy realised that he'd seen the boy, but he seemed not to mind. In fact, it was as if he was waiting for Simba to join him.

Then she heard the boy begin to make soft, gentle noises.

'He's talking to the cub!' James breathed.

'Shh!' Joseph said.

Simba put his stick down. He squatted close to the ground, speaking slowly.

Mandy stared in amazement as the cub raised himself. He arched his back, then rested on his haunches to stretch and yawn. Then he trotted swiftly up to the boy.

Simba reached out one hand. The cub nuzzled up to him. The boy lowered his head and the two of them rubbed foreheads. They heard the purr of the lion and the boy's gentle whisper.

James's mouth had fallen open. Mandy's eyes were wide, as Simba fondled the cub without fear. And now he reached for something which he kept under his red cloak. They saw the cub sniff at a leather bag which was tightly bound with string.

Joseph grinned and relaxed. 'Meat,' he explained as the boy opened the bag. 'The young one has smelled it.'

And sure enough the cub wove between Simba's legs, his tail up, rubbing against him. The boy drew the meat from the bag. The cub seized it, carried it a safe distance and began to tear it with his sharp teeth.

'He's hungry.' Joseph nodded with satisfaction. 'Feed well, little one!'

Fascinated, Mandy saw Simba squat once more and wait while the lion fed. 'Shall we fetch the crate now?' she whispered.

The old man nodded. 'Bring it here.'

So they ran to the jeep and unloaded the large wooden box. By the time they brought it back, the cub had devoured his food. He sat close to Simba, licking his paws and grooming himself.

Mandy beamed at James. 'Just like a kitten!' The cub rubbed the back of his wet paw over his face and behind his ears.

'Grown-up lions are supposed to be kings of the jungle, aren't they? So he must be the prince!' James was out of breath as they rested the crate on the ground.

'What shall we call him?' Mandy was so thrilled that she forgot to lower her voice.

'How about Safi? It's what they say round here when you ask them how they are. You know; "*Habari*?" – "How are you?" And they say "*Safi*", meaning "Good".'

'Safi?' She studied the cub, then nodded. 'It suits him.'

The cub stopped grooming and pricked his ears. Suddenly he grew wary.

Simba glared at Mandy and James. Then he fixed his gaze on the crate. He picked up his stick and stood up straight, folding his robe across his shoulder once more.

'What's he doing now?' James asked.

Simba stared at the box. He said a few words to the cub; a short command. The young lion growled and retreated behind him. The boy gave another sharp order and the lion turned away.

'No, wait!' Mandy called. 'Don't let him go! We want to rescue him and take him to the mountains!' She began to follow Safi.

But Simba stepped in front of her. He called over his shoulder and the lion began to run, heading swiftly along the shore, making for the same tree as yesterday. He loped easily, not looking back.

Mandy stopped. She was face to face with the boy. 'We only want to save him!' she pleaded. Behind her she heard James and Joseph dragging the crate, hurrying to join her.

Simba shook his head. 'He likes to be free.'

'I know. But we only have to put him in the cage for a few hours. We want to drive him up to the mountains and set him free again!' She looked desperately beyond Simba. Safi had reached the tree and now he sprang into it. He reached the lowest branch with one easy leap. Soon his speckled shape disappeared amongst the leaves.

'No!' The word came from deep in the boy's

throat. He stared angrily at them.

'But you don't understand! If he stays here, the other animals will hunt him and kill him!' Mandy tried to dodge past, desperate to go and tempt the cub down from the tree.

Once more Simba barred her way. He planted his staff wide across her path. His eyes drilled into her with their intense stare.

She felt Joseph draw back. She struggled for a moment to pass by, then turned to plead with their driver. 'Tell him; explain that Safi will die if he stays here!'

But the old man drew her away. He warned James not to disobey the boy. 'Simba knows. He's the lion's friend. We must do as he says.'

In the end there was nothing they could do. The sun beat down, the land shimmered in the heat. Mandy felt dizzy and helpless.

'Come on,' James said at last. The cub had vanished high into the tree. Simba would never let them get near him now. 'We'll have to go back and tell the others.'

As he and Joseph picked up the crate and made for the jeep, Mandy's shoulders sagged. She felt her lips tremble as she begged with her eyes one last time for Simba's help.

He stared coldly back.

He didn't understand. Mandy dropped her head to avoid his gaze. Then, with hot tears stinging her eyes, she turned to join the others.

Four

'I'm so sorry.' Levina put her arm round Mandy's shoulder. She'd come out on to the veranda when she heard the jeep return to Kampi ya Simba. She knew from Mandy's face that the rescue hadn't gone according to plan.

James filled in the details while Joseph unloaded the empty crate.

Mandy could hear her mother talking on the radio link inside the office. Across the yard she heard the hiss of water in the shower hut and her father's yells as the cold spray drenched him.

'Perhaps you could go back later and try again,' Levina suggested.

'Not if Simba is there,' James said flatly. He flopped on to the step, his hands hanging between his knees. 'No way will he let us get anywhere near.'

'But he can't stay for ever. He has to go home sometime.' Their friend tried to look on the bright side.

'Yes, but by then Safi could be anywhere.' He was as frustrated as Mandy. Why hadn't the boy been willing to listen to their plan? He turned to Levina. 'We thought he'd want to help.'

'He probably does,' she insisted. She looked thoughtfully at the two disappointed faces. 'Look, Simba knows about the problems that the lion-cub faces. As a matter of fact, no one knows them better.' She explained carefully, taking her time.

'Then why didn't he understand about the crate?' Mandy sighed. 'Surely he realises he can't go on feeding the cub for ever. Sooner or later he'll have to leave him alone out there. Then what will happen?' They'd been so near to carrying out the rescue. It was only the Masai boy who had stopped them.

Levina echoed her sigh. 'He understood.'

'Then why?'

'I don't know why. But you can be sure that Simba knew what he was doing. If he didn't think that taking the lion by crate was a good idea, then I would trust that decision. I've known the boy for a long time. When it comes to lions, he's never wrong.'

Mandy frowned as James took up the argument. 'That's all very well. Nobody likes putting an animal in a cage. We only wanted to do it to save Safi's life. And anyway, it's not as if Simba came up with a better idea, is it? He just sent the cub up a tree. Now we're stuck.'

'Trust him,' Levina said again, looking round with a smile as Adam Hope set up a wail from inside the shower hut. He shuffled and banged about, then emerged dripping wet, shampoo streaming down his face. He had a towel wrapped round his waist and he walked with his eyes shut, holding his arms out in front like a blind man.

'Ouch!' he cried as he stepped on a thorn. 'Ooch! Ouch!' He hobbled on, straight into a guy-rope on one of the tents. He tripped and stumbled, then regained his balance. 'Help! The water went off and I've got soap in my eyes!'

In spite of everything, Mandy couldn't stop a smile from spreading over her face. 'Wait there!' she called. She dashed across the yard to fiddle with the shower tap. 'You're right, the water's run out!' Grabbing a dry towel from the rail, she ran out to help.

'Run out?' Adam Hope fumbled with the towel. 'How can it have run out? I was in the middle of my shower!' He rubbed his eyes. When he opened them, he saw Mandy, James and Levina all grinning at him.

'Very easily,' Levina said sweetly. 'This is Africa, remember. Here the water is uncertain. You might say it's temperamental!'

By now Mandy's mum had come out of the office. 'That's not my husband you're talking about, is it?' She laughed at the sight of him covered in shampoo. The towel round his waist was beginning to loosen and slip.

He hitched it back up. 'Very funny,' he muttered. But then he began to smile too. 'Well, I suppose I could always go and take a dip in the lake to wash the soap off.'

'The crocodiles would like that.' Levina's mouth twitched.

'On second thoughts . . .' He looked round helplessly.

'Listen!' James could hear the pipe in the shower hut begin to rattle and groan. There was a sloshing noise from the water tank above, then a fresh burst of what sounded like rain. 'Quick, it's started up again!'

So Mandy's dad rushed back to finish his shower, while Levina and Emily Hope stayed to cheer James and Mandy up.

'I think your idea about going back to look for the cub again is good,' Mrs Hope said. 'Perhaps first thing tomorrow morning?' She shaded her eyes and looked out over the sun scorched plain.

Levina said nothing. She went inside to fetch cold drinks.

'Will you and Dad come with us?' True to her nature, Mandy refused to be beaten. Though they'd been disappointed today, they must try again tomorrow. 'Maybe you could fix up to bring a tranquilliser dart from your vets' bag. We could use it to get Safi safely into the crate.'

Her mum bit her top lip. 'That sounds rather extreme.'

'But Safi is in a life or death situation out there,' James pointed out. 'Think about it. It's true he had something to eat today, thanks to

Simba. So he's not going to starve. But that doesn't mean he's safe from the hyenas and everything else. And he isn't learning to hunt for himself.'

By this time Mandy's dad had rejoined them, fresh from the shower. He towelled his hair, then nodded. 'James is right. And now that we know that the little chap sticks close to the lake, we can drive across tomorrow and track him down. I think we should take some meat as bait.'

'You make it sound simple,' Levina warned. She brought the tray of drinks with her.

'Well, I know we're no lion experts,' Adam Hope admitted. 'But if he's hungry, he should take the bait.'

'*If.*' Their friend repeated the word several times. '*If* he's hungry. *If* Simba doesn't feed him again . . . *If* he stays in the same place . . .' She put her head to one side and spoke kindly. 'I'm only trying to say that your plan might not work. This *is* Africa, remember!'

Africa. In the lazy heat of the afternoon sun, Mandy and James kept to the shade. They went into the office and helped Levina to track the paths of the lion prides that had been shipped off to the Ruwenzori Mountains.

The radio tags were working well, sending clear signals that allowed them to stick pins in a map to locate their exact position. For the signals from the first pride they used white pins, for the second set of signals they used blue, and for the third pride they used red.

'See how they're marking out their new territory.' Levina showed them the clearly coloured areas on the map. 'Matthew Mulakesi was careful to take them to a fresh place where there were no lions present. Now they can settle there in peace.' She sounded satisfied as she switched off the radio and looked at her watch. 'Time for Joseph to drive me to Arusha,' she announced. 'This evening we must stay in town, and in the morning we must buy food. Would you two like to come?'

'No, thanks.' Mandy shook her head. The trip would involve a long drive across wild country; perhaps a chance to see elephants and giraffes on the way. But it also meant they would be away from camp overnight, which would ruin their plan to rescue the cub in the morning.

'No, thanks,' James echoed. 'I'll stay here.'

Mandy smiled at him. Safi came first with him too.

So Levina and Joseph loaded one of the jeeps with crates of empty bottles and set off for town, leaving the Hopes and James with Thomas. Evening shadows had begun to creep across the valley, the heat was fading. A pink tinge appeared in the sky as the jeep climbed the rocky mountain track out of the crater, raising a trail of dust behind it.

'Perfect!' Adam Hope said with a sigh. He and Emily Hope were sitting on the veranda peeling potatoes for supper. There was no sound except for the birdsong in the evening air.

Mandy and James had wandered a little way out of camp; just far enough to see the shore of the lake stretching northwards.

'I wonder if Simba is still keeping guard,' James murmured.

'Me too.' Mandy tried to pick out the crimson figure. Squinting, she thought she could see the fan-shaped thorntree, the clump of nearby rocks. But there was no sign of the boy. 'I hope Safi's safe.'

'Uh-oh, visitors!' James pointed to the west. Three thin trails of dust approached the camp.

'I wonder who that is.' Mandy was surprised to see three cars all at once. Evening was drawing in fast as the jeeps drew near. Unlike at home, where they had gentle dusks, here, darkness would fall as soon as the sun went down behind the hills.

Two of the cars slowed down, but one drove at speed straight for the camp. It scattered a herd of gazelles.

Mandy and James ran to tell the others. 'We've got visitors!' James called. Thomas looked up from his cooking pots, Emily and Adam Hope came down from the veranda.

The car came into the yard. A man dressed in a fawn safari suit and heavy boots jumped to the ground. He slammed the door and strode across. 'Where's Dr Lemiso?' he asked Thomas.

'Gone,' the boy said. There was no '*Jambo*' or smile of welcome for this hasty visitor.

'Gone where?' The man stared rudely at James and Mandy. Then he spotted Mr and Mrs Hope. 'I'm Larry Southall,' he announced. 'I manage the farm at Kijano to the west of here. I need to have a word with someone about a lion-cub that's on the loose.'

Adam Hope came forward and introduced

himself. 'We already know about the lion, thanks,' he said pleasantly.

Mandy studied the visitor. He was stockily built, with a broad leather belt round his thick waist. He wore a cap to shade his sunburned face. His ginger hair was short, his mouth thin under a straight, narrow nose. A farmer from the west – this must be one of the men who had a licence to shoot the lions!

'Then you know there's been a foul-up,' he told Mandy's dad. 'Those do-gooding wardens rounded the prides up before we could get at them. But they left a young one behind, and now it's been seen bothering my cattle.'

'When?' Emily Hope interrupted the bad-tempered account.

'Last night. The night before that it was seen over at Bill Irvine's place. Before too long it'll take one of our young cows, you mark my words.'

'But it's only a cub, isn't it?'

'All the more reason to deal with it fast. The young ones are the worst. They maul an animal without finishing it off properly because they don't have the strength or the skill. When we find it in the morning we have to finish the job off ourselves. These cubs can cost us a fortune if we're not careful.'

Mandy listened in dismay. The man, Larry Southall, talked about killing the lion-cub as if it was all in a day's work.

'Has it been seen round the camp?' he demanded now.

Mandy's dad cleared his throat. He glanced at her. 'No. The cub hasn't been anywhere near here.'

She breathed a sigh of relief, trying to outstare the man's curious gaze.

'No, well you've just arrived, haven't you? You wouldn't know what to look out for.' He turned to Thomas. 'What about you? Have you seen this cub?'

Thomas shook his head, suddenly busy again with the fire and the pans.

'Hmm.' Larry Southall looked suspiciously round. 'Bill Irvine's got a jeep out, and I've brought two from my place. Sooner or later we'll spot him.'

Mr Hope looked round at the setting sun. 'Not before nightfall, surely?'

'Maybe not.' The farm manager sniffed and turned away. 'But I'll put an armed guard on my herd tonight, I'm telling you that for a start. I can't take chances. And neither will my neighbour if he's got any sense.'

Mandy clenched her jaw to stop herself from answering back. '*Go away! Go away!*' she said under her breath. The man's broad back showed a band of wet through his pale shirt where he'd sweated as he drove. His neck bristled with short ginger hairs. '*And don't ever come back!*'

He walked off and climbed into his jeep. 'Tell Dr Lemiso I dropped by, and that I got that permit. She'll take sides with the wardens, of course, but you can let her know we're properly licensed now!'

'I will,' Adam Hope said calmly.

The jeep roared back into life. As he drove away, Larry Southall leaned out with a final warning. 'And tell her we'll be back first thing in the morning,' he called. 'And we'll be fully armed!'

Five

Darkness fell quickly in the Ruwenzori Crater. Sitting on the veranda in the light of a paraffin lamp, Mandy and James tried to decide what to do next.

'We have to get there first,' she insisted. The farmers had driven off across the plain, their headlights fading into the distance. Now the whole valley was still and black.

'OK, it's a race,' James agreed, his voice tense. 'Hey, Mandy, are you all right?'

She nodded. 'Why?'

'Your face looks weird.'

'Thanks!' She pushed her fair hair behind her ears and tried to grin back at James. 'Yours doesn't look too hot either!' The lamp cast its long shadows, making his nose look bigger. The flame's reflection glittered in the lenses of his glasses.

'Time for bed, you two!' Adam Hope called out from inside his tent. 'You have to be up early in the morning, remember. Anyway, we've said all there is to say!' They'd talked for hours about how they could save the cub.

Mandy's mum emerged from the shower hut carrying a torch. She joined them on the veranda before she too turned in for the night. 'Let's go through it one more time,' she said gently. 'The plan is to get up before dawn, at about six. We should be ready to go at first light, and since we live nearer to the lake than the men from the farms, we should get there first. With a bit of luck, we'll spot the cub and be out of there before they even show up. OK?'

They nodded. Mrs Hope stooped to kiss Mandy good night. 'Try not to worry. And ask Thomas to turn out the light when he goes to bed, would you?' She yawned and headed for the tent. 'We'll see you both bright and early.'

James stared at Mandy across the small table where they sat. Inside the hut, Thomas was writing a letter to his family in Arusha. 'What's wrong?' James knew they couldn't just switch off and go to bed. Mandy looked too keyed up.

She sighed. 'How will we find Safi?' She pictured them setting out in the jeep at dawn across the vast crater. 'Where do we start?'

'Near the tree where we last saw him, I guess.'

'And what if he isn't there?' Without Joseph to guide them they stood less chance, she knew.

He shrugged. 'You think we need help?'

'Yes.' There was silence. A large brown moth flew towards the light and fluttered close to the flame. 'And you know who from,' she whispered.

'Simba?'

'Yes.' The lion-boy would be sure to find Safi faster than anyone.

'Mandy, don't even think about it!' James scraped his chair back and stood up. 'It won't work. Simba is never going to agree to help us, not now that he knows we want to put Safi in a crate.'

'But if we tell him there are men coming with guns!' Mandy whispered urgently. 'He doesn't know *that*, does he?'

'When? How can we tell him? We don't even know where he lives.'

'No, but I bet Thomas does.' She glanced inside the hut. The boy's head was bowed over the table. He was still hard at work. 'We could ask him to show us.'

James stopped to think. 'Will there be enough time?'

'Who knows? But if Thomas does show us Simba's place, we could ask him for help. Then we can all drive straight down to the lake and we might still get there before the farmers. What do you think?'

'It's a big risk.'

'As big a risk as trying to find Safi by ourselves?' She thought of the cub out there alone under the moon and stars.

'OK.' James set his mouth in a determined line. 'It's worth a try. Let's go in and ask!'

Their cook looked up and greeted their request with a frown. 'Yes, I know Simba's house,' he told them. He sat with his pen poised over the paper; a boy of about fifteen who was feeling homesick and writing a letter to his parents in the city. 'His *boma* is near here.'

'*Boma*?' Mandy asked.

'His village. It is beyond the big baobab tree on the hill.'

'And please could you take us there tomorrow at dawn?'

Thomas listened to their reasons. He tapped his pen on the table. 'It's a Masai village,' he reminded them. 'I am not Masai.' He reminded them that he came from far away, from a big town three hundred kilometres to the south.

'But you can speak Swahili,' James said. 'You'll be able to tell Simba about the farmers and their guns.'

Thomas explained with a shake of his head. 'The language isn't the problem. But the Masai are a proud people. It's true they don't like the farmers. But they don't like our camps either. They say they were the first ones to live here by Lake Kasanka. The land belongs to them.' Thomas folded his letter as Mandy and James waited nervously for an answer.

'It could be Safi's only chance of being saved,' Mandy urged. 'Everyone says that Simba can get lions to do what he tells them. And I'm sure the Masai people will listen. Please, Thomas, we really need your help.'

The boy looked steadily at her. He tutted and lifted his head with a short jerk. 'I will be ready at dawn,' he agreed at last. He put the letter in an envelope and sealed it. 'We can go to the *boma*. We can try!'

Simba's village was built in the shade of some thorntrees, beyond the ancient baobab on the hill behind the camp. The squat, thick tree with its twisted trunk and stunted branches kept the entrance to the *boma* well hidden. Emily Hope drove the jeep up there in the pale dawn light, and no one saw the huts until they were almost upon them. Thomas pointed them out and told her to stop.

The dozen or so round houses formed a circle inside a barrier of thorny branches, cut down and stacked to form a rough fence. The huts were tiny, with straw roofs. There were no windows, and no chimneys; only a small doorway leading into a dark interior. As their jeep pulled up nearby, Mandy saw a tall figure come out of one of the huts and pass through a gap in the fence.

'Ready?' Thomas climbed down and beckoned Mandy.

'Take care,' Emily Hope said. She gripped the steering wheel and peered out at the simple village.

'You're sure you don't want us to come along

too?' Mr Hope asked for the last time.

'No, thanks.' Thomas had told them it was better for Mandy to come alone with him into the *boma* to find Simba. He led the way to meet the man at the gate.

'We're here if you need us,' Mandy's dad said.

From the back seat of the jeep, James gave Mandy a thumbs-up sign.

Mandy smiled, then followed Thomas and their guide through the gate.

She braced herself as the Masai people came out of their huts in twos and threes to stare at the white girl dressed in T-shirt and shorts. Women dressed in bright robes stood watching, their ears hung with rings of beads and silver. Children sat cross-legged on the ground, or hid behind the women. A group of young men gathered beneath a tree. No one spoke.

They stopped outside the biggest hut. An old man came out as their guide stepped to one side.

'*Jambo*,' Thomas said warily. He nudged Mandy to give the same greeting.

'*Jambo*.' She found her voice at last.

The old man stared intently at her. Then he broke the silence with a nod of his head and a single word. '*Karibu*.'

'What does he say?' Mandy whispered to Thomas. The strange sounds meant nothing.

'He says "Welcome". This is the chief of the village.' Thomas raised his hand in greeting. '*Habari*? How are you?'

'*Safi.*'

'He says he's well,' Thomas reported.

Mandy gave a sigh of relief. The ice was broken and the Masais had accepted their visit. 'Ask him where we can find Simba,' she urged.

Thomas began a stream of words. The chief listened. Still the other men kept their distance and the women shielded their children. Thomas listened to the old man's reply, then turned to Mandy.

'The boy is with the goats,' he told her. 'His job is to take them out for the day to graze in the valley.'

Mandy looked round to see a smaller compound within the village fence. There were dozens of goats; black, brown and cream, all jostling and bleating as the sun rose. Then she saw a figure opening up the gate to let them out. This must be Simba setting out on his day's work. 'Ask if another boy can look after the goats,' she pleaded. 'Tell him we have to save the lion-cub from the farmers!'

Thomas spoke again. The old man listened. He glanced from Mandy to the jeep standing outside the fence. He spoke rapidly to Thomas.

'He says the boy has spoken of you already. He doesn't want to help you.'

Mandy frowned. 'Tell him we don't mean the lion any harm. Tell him about the farmers and their guns!' She clenched her hands and waited.

The headman listened once more, then clicked his tongue. He narrowed his eyes and looked down into the valley. Then he gave an order. One of the young men broke away from his group. He went to fetch Simba.

'The old man doesn't like the farmers,' Thomas explained. 'He doesn't like their fat cattle eating the grass in the valley. And he doesn't like their guns.' He smiled encouragement at Mandy. 'Look; here's Simba.'

And now, as the lion-boy came near, an interested crowd drew round Mandy, Thomas and the chief. People began to listen and murmur until Mandy couldn't bear the confusion of voices any longer.

'We have to save the cub!' She spoke above the crowd.

Simba gazed at her. 'To put him in a cage?' he said scornfully, in slow but clear English.

'No. To take him to the mountains. Otherwise they'll shoot him. Don't you see?'

'I see that your plan is no good,' Simba replied. 'To put him in a cage and take him in a car? Will he know that you want to help him? Will he want to go with you? No, he'll try to escape. And if you force him, you'll become his enemy.'

'It's for his own good.' She lowered her voice. Time was slipping away. 'What else can we do?'

'There are other ways. You can win his trust,' Simba said simply.

'How?' Somehow, Mandy believed him instantly. He spoke as if he knew all the ways of the lions, and how best to reunite the cub with his pride.

'Feed him and talk with him. Hunt with him, sleep with him. Take care of him as his own family would.' Simba described the way he would do it. 'I would find him and make the journey to the mountains on foot.'

'Walk there?' Mandy gasped. It was a distance of forty kilometres or more, through the bush and who knew what dangers!

'Yes, and when I reached the mountains I would find his family and return him to them. Only then could we be sure that we'd saved him.

With your way we could not be sure.'

'"We"?' Mandy looked straight into Simba's dark brown eyes. 'Does that mean you'll let us help?'

'Maybe.' The boy turned away and spoke to the chief. Mandy asked Thomas to translate what he said.

'First he must ask the old man's permission,' Thomas said. 'And the head of the village says that your father and mother must be brought here and told of the plan.'

A man went out through the gate. Soon Mr and Mrs Hope and James came hurrying in.

'But he's thinking about it?' Mandy closed her eyes and tilted her head back. A fantastic journey across the crater, leading Safi back to his pride; it was beyond her wildest dreams!

As the villagers made way for the three new visitors, stepping aside to let them into the centre of the crowd, Thomas told Mandy what the old man had decided. 'He wants Simba to try and save the lion-cub.'

'Wonderful!' Mandy drew a deep breath. 'And can we go too?' She knew that she and James had put their faith in Simba and altered their own plans to fit in with his. She only hoped that her mum and dad would see it the same way.

And now there were more minutes slipping by as Mandy's parents met the head of the village. The sun rose over the horizon while Mr and Mrs Hope listened to the new, exciting plan.

'The journey will take two, maybe three days,' Thomas explained. 'They'll walk in the morning and in the evening. At noon they will rest.'

Adam Hope listened with a serious expression. 'How difficult will it be?' he asked.

'Much walking,' Simba said. 'But the land by the lake is flat. Not too difficult.'

Mandy stood by James, gazing at her mum and dad. 'Please!' She couldn't say any more. Her throat was dry, she clenched her hands tight.

'And how dangerous is it?' Emily Hope wanted to know.

Simba shrugged. 'There's no danger for me.' It was his everyday life; walking in the bush, being with the animals. 'And so there's no danger for these two if they follow me.'

Mandy's mum and dad considered it carefully.

'Wouldn't it be great?' she whispered to James.

'Yes, if Simba can actually get Safi to follow us!' He didn't sound so sure that it would work.

'He will if we take food and help him to hunt. Safi trusts Simba, remember.' She reminded him that yesterday the cub had done exactly as the boy had asked.

James nodded. 'Yes. It *would* be fantastic!'

They turned to Mr and Mrs Hope for their long-awaited answer.

'There's just one more thing.' Adam Hope had seen a new snag. 'What about the farmers? They're probably on the cub's trail right this minute.'

'Ah, yes.' Mandy's mum folded her arms and looked serious. 'We wouldn't want anyone to get into their line of fire by mistake. That would be dreadful.'

'They could shoot first and ask questions later,' Mr Hope pointed out.

His wife nodded. 'They want that lion-cub. That's all they're bothered about.'

'You're right.' He'd weighed things up and made his decision.

Mandy knew the answer before he said it. She could tell by the way he turned away from her to speak to Simba. 'We think your idea is too dangerous,' he said quietly. 'I'm sorry; there's no way we can let Mandy and James go with you.'

Six

'See!' Adam Hope stood beside the jeep outside the Masai village. He pointed to a trail of dust to the west of the lake. 'It's a good job we didn't let you two go ahead. Larry Southall warned us they'd be back.'

Mandy made out the three jeeps. She hardly cared now that the farmers would reach the lake before they did, for the headman of the village had also reconsidered his decision. In the light of Mr and Mrs Hope's worries, he too had forbidden Simba from setting out. Now no one had permission to go and rescue Safi. She gazed beyond the valley to the Ruwenzori hills.

James came up quietly beside her. 'You're not

going to give up, are you?' The villagers had come out to watch the jeeps. They were surrounded by the silent men and the murmuring women.

Mandy looked at the ground. She dug her toe underneath a stone and kicked it loose. 'What can we do? You heard what Mum and Dad said.'

'Yep, and they're probably right.'

Mandy frowned. 'You're not supposed to agree with them!'

James shrugged. 'Anyway, I've got a kind of feeling . . .' He urged her to take a look at the Masais.

'What . . . ?' The villagers were beginning to move off down the hill. The young men went first, Simba amongst them, striding ahead. The women and older men held the children's hands and went more slowly into the valley.

'Mmm.' Emily Hope looked on shrewdly. 'I see what James means.'

From their high vantage point, they saw how the villagers had reached the plain and begun to gather there. There were forty, maybe fifty of them altogether. No one spoke; they simply looked.

'They're waiting for the jeeps!' Mandy said. 'Thomas, what are they planning to do?'

'Nothing,' he said slowly.

For some reason Mandy felt her heartbeat quicken. It was true, the Masai people weren't *doing* anything. They stood in silence, as was their way, some leaning on long staffs, all facing the oncoming cars. 'What happens when Mr Southall sees them?' she asked.

'It looks like he already has.' Her father pointed to where the three cars had screeched to a halt. They were about three hundred metres from the villagers. As the trail of dust settled, no one moved. The jeeps sat glinting in the sun. The Masai men stood and faced them. There was silence.

Then someone broke from the crowd and came running back up the hill shouting in Swahili.

'It's Simba.' James recognised him. 'He wants us to go down.'

They turned to Thomas. 'Is it safe?' Emily Hope asked. 'This isn't going to turn nasty, is it?'

'No. He says they need you to talk to the farmers.' Thomas didn't seem surprised. He led the way down the rocky slope.

They decided to follow, listening to Simba's explanation as they went.

'My people refuse to speak to the men, but the drivers won't dare to pass. We need your father to speak for us. They'll listen to him.'

'You bet they will!' Mr Hope joined the Masai ranks. They towered above him, standing without speaking, all gazing in the direction of the unwelcome jeeps. 'And so would I too, if I was faced with this lot!'

Mandy ran to keep up with her father and Simba. 'What do you want Dad to tell them?' she gasped. Larry Southall had climbed down from his jeep. He left the door swinging and came to meet them, a shotgun under his arm.

'Can you tell them to call off this hunt?' Simba asked. 'Will they take their guns back to their farms? Then there will be no lion hunt.'

Adam Hope nodded. 'I'll do what I can.'

'Mandy!' Mrs Hope called her back. 'It might not be safe!'

'Dad, can I come?' She appealed to be allowed to go.

He paused and called back to his wife. 'It's OK, I'll look after her. Come on!'

Simba had stridden ahead. But now, a few metres from Mr Southall, he stopped.

Quickly they joined him.

'What brings you out here so early, as if I

didn't know!' The farm manager looked at Mr Hope and tried to sound casual, but he didn't succeed. He glanced over their shoulders at the gathered tribesmen. 'What's up? Have they found the lion?'

'No. Have you?' Mandy's dad met Southall's gaze.

'Not yet. But we will.' He tapped the barrel of his gun.

'What if we told you we had a better idea?'

Mandy stood tall and proud beside her father. He sounded calm and reasonable.

'Such as?'

'Such as you calling off the hunt and letting Simba here find the cub.'

'Then what?'

'He reckons he can lead him to the national park to join the rest of his pride.'

The farm manager gave a snort. 'And the moon's made of cheese!'

'He can!' Mandy protested. 'We've seen him talk to the cub. He can tell him what to do!'

'Over my dead body!' Southall sneered. 'You don't expect me to believe that?'

'Maybe not. But the villagers back there reckon he can do it too.' Mr Hope gestured over his shoulder. 'In fact, they seem to think it's by far the best idea. The only thing is, we want to be sure there are no accidental shootings. That's why we want you to back off for a while.' He looked steadily at the angry man.

'And what about our cattle? What happens if this kid can't do what he says? Who'll pay for the damage?'

'I will.'

Mandy stared up at her father.

'You?' It stopped Southall in his tracks.

He nodded. 'If this cub attacks any of your cattle, or Mr Irvine's, or anyone else's for that matter, I'll pay for you to buy new stock, OK?'

The farm manager stared. 'You'd put your faith in a fourteen-year-old kid?'

'I sure would.' He didn't hesitate.

'And what if we refuse? We have a licence to go ahead and shoot this cub, you know.'

Mandy could see the manager keeping one wary eye on the Masais. Guns or no guns, she knew the men could be forced to back off.

Mr Hope held firm. 'Look, it's not the best option, believe me. I'm a vet. I can't stand around and see a magnificent animal needlessly destroyed; not when there's another way out. And I do believe the boy has a special way with these cats. From what Mandy has told me about him, I think you should give him a chance. At least let them try.'

Still Southall tried to save face. He screwed up his eyes and made a sucking noise through his teeth. 'If I agree, it's not got anything to do with that lot over there.' He pointed to the villagers, massed together in their crimson cloaks. 'It's because I'm taking a vet's expert opinion, right?'

'Right.' Mr Hope moved quickly to shake hands. 'So you'll move off. Simba says he'll need three days.'

'One.'

Mr Hope glanced at Simba. The boy shook his head.

'Two.' Southall made it sound like his best offer.

'Isn't that long enough?' Mandy whispered anxiously. She didn't think the farmers could be pushed to give them any more.

'Three days,' Simba said again.

'OK. But after that, it'll be open season. If they haven't got the cub into the park by Saturday, we can go ahead and do it our way!' Southall's face was red with anger, but he was helpless.

'Fair enough,' Mandy's dad agreed. 'But for

three days none of you comes near.'

They'd made a deal. The farm manager hunched his shoulders and went back to the jeeps to break the news.

Mandy gave her father a hug, then ran to her mum and James. 'Did you see that?' she cried. 'Wasn't Dad great?'

'It was nothing.' Adam Hope came up. He was blushing. 'I didn't do anything. It was Simba and these people here . . .'

They looked around to include the Masai people in their congratulations. But the men, women and children were fading away in a flurry of dust. Having done what they had set out to do, they were leaving; some to herd the goats, some to trek to the lake for water, some to go to school. The Hopes, James and Thomas stood alone.

'Where's Simba?' Mandy said. He too had vanished.

'Gone to get ready,' Thomas told them. 'He says you should meet him by the lake in one hour.'

Seven

'Take this with you.' Emily Hope handed Levina's portable radio transmitter to James as they got ready to set off. 'Put it in your rucksack. Then we'll be able to keep in touch.'

'Don't worry, we'll be OK.' Mandy strapped her sleeping bag to her rucksack. Her fingers tugged clumsily at the buckles in her hurry to be gone.

'But we *will* worry; that's what parents are for!' Mrs Hope made them listen to her instructions. 'I want you to call us each day at twelve noon and each evening at six. Then we can be sure you're safe. And this evening I want Simba to take you to the next research station along the lake. It's called Zebra Camp. Levina's colleague, Charles Tawana, has said you can spend the night there. I've already called him to arrange it.'

'Mu-um!' Mandy struggled to hitch her rucksack on to her shoulders.

'I don't want any arguments, Mandy. Either you do it this way or not at all.' She didn't have to raise her voice to make herself perfectly clear.

Mandy recognised the tone. 'OK, I promise.'

'And no going off by yourselves,' Adam Hope reminded them. 'And no having bright ideas and ignoring what Simba tells you to do; got it?'

'Yep.' James agreed to be careful.

'Right then, gee-up! What are we waiting for?' Mandy's dad got them moving. 'Simba gave you an hour. Have you got everything?'

'Emergency food?' Emily Hope asked.

'Yep.' They had biscuits, dried fruit and chocolate.

'Plenty to drink?'

'Yep.' James held up his water-bottle.

'First-aid kit? Spare T-shirt and shorts? Toothbrush?'

'Yep, yep, and yep.'

Mandy and James were ready. They climbed

into the jeep and waved goodbye to Thomas.

'We're not fussing, are we?' Mr Hope said as he took the wheel.

'Yep,' Mandy grinned. 'But that's what parents are for!'

They were off at last. They arrived at their meeting place in time to see Simba reach there on foot. Not for him the carefully packed rucksack and sleeping bag; he stood as before, his red robe draped across his shoulder, empty handed except for his stick.

Mandy and James stepped down to meet him. They heard the engine whine and the tyres crunch over the stones, ready to return the way it had come.

'Look after them for us!' Mandy's mum called to the lion-boy.

He nodded solemnly.

'Good luck!' Adam Hope gave them a thumbs-up sign. Then they were gone.

'*Jambo*!' Simba greeted them quietly and told them that they had arrived at a good moment.

'Have you seen Safi?' Mandy scanned the shore for the cub.

'His prints; here, by the water.' He stooped to show them round marks in the soft earth.

'How recent are they?' James asked as he and

Mandy crouched to examine them. The prints led into the cool, clear water, then came out again a few metres away. They went up the bank then disappeared in a scuffle of large hoof-prints. It seemed that the cub had come to drink, but there was no telling where he was now.

'One, maybe two hours old. Just after daybreak.' Simba stood up straight. 'There were zebra here too. Maybe he tried to hunt one.' He grinned at the scuff marks on the shore. 'But he was too slow.'

'How can you tell?' Mandy asked.

'No blood,' came the simple answer. 'The cub must hunt something small, not zebra.' He turned and cut away across a patch of grass and low bushes, pointing at a tuft of fawn fur caught on a branch. 'He came this way.'

Simba showed James and Mandy how to pick up the trail. There were more prints beyond the bushes, then an area of flattened grass beside a rock. 'This is where he rested,' Simba said.

Mandy could already feel the heat of the sun on her shoulders. She pulled her cap down to shade her eyes. 'Will he be hungry again?' she whispered. Safi could be anywhere; behind the next bush, up the next tree. They mustn't startle him by calling too loudly or stumbling against a hidden stone.

'He's always hungry,' came the reply. Simba listened, then he began to run swiftly towards a high ledge of rock. Mandy and James followed more slowly. By the time they reached the ledge, Simba had already climbed it and was gazing back down at the lake.

'Too late,' he reported. 'But he was here.'

'How do you know?' James was mystified once more.

'Magic!' Mandy said with a grin. 'He just knows!' She recalled how he'd appeared out of nowhere when they first met.

Simba tutted. 'Not magic. Here's blood.' He pointed to bright red spots glistening on the rock.

Mandy drew breath. 'What did he kill?'

'Hyrax. Small creature like a rat. The taste is no good.' Simba pulled a face and made a spitting noise. 'The cub has taken his kill away, but he won't eat it.'

'Where is he now?' Mandy hadn't heard a sound, yet Simba had actually managed to pinpoint where the cub had been hunting.

'By the water.' He pointed to the north.

'Can you see him?' James clambered on to the ledge to look.

'No. But watch those birds moving away from the shore.'

'Because of Safi?' Mandy had joined them in time to see a flock of pink birds flutter and stride from the water's edge. Her voice gathered urgency as she strained to look. 'What should we do now?'

For Simba the question was too simple. Instead of giving an answer, he jumped silently from the ledge and ran towards the lake. He stopped by a tree and took his leather bag from under his cloak. 'Hyrax is no good,' he repeated. 'This is better.'

He drew meat from the bag and offered it to Mandy.

'You want me to take it to him?' she gasped.

Simba nodded. 'So he can learn to trust you.' Impatiently he pushed the meat into her hands.

She felt her stomach churn, but she took it, knowing that Simba was right. 'Where is he? I can't see him.' The light from the shining lake dazzled her.

'Walk to the water. Put the meat on the ground. Wait. The cub will come.'

Mandy nodded and set off on her mission.

She knew each step was vital. Somewhere, unseen by them, Safi lay and watched. If she moved suddenly, if her nerve failed, she would scare him off.

At last she reached the salty rim of the lake and put the meat down. Careful not to jerk or stumble, she eased back a few steps. Then she crouched and waited, resting the palms of her hands on the warm pebbles.

After five long minutes, Safi crept out from behind a bush. Mandy saw the flamingos look up and flap their wings. Then she saw the low, speckled shape leave the shadows and prowl across the shore. Lifting one heavy paw after another, he moved stealthily towards the gift of meat, never for a moment taking his eyes off Mandy.

She held her breath, struck once more by the cub's beauty. His fur was soft and thick, the rims of his golden eyes marked out with black. The brown rosettes speckled his tawny head and back.

He moved without a sound, ears pricked, whiskers twitching. Then he pounced at the meat. He sank his claws and teeth into the flesh. Mandy steeled herself to watch, knowing that she must not disturb him.

When the cub had almost devoured the meat, she felt, rather than heard, Simba come up from behind.

'Good.' He stood beside her, watching the cub who saw him for the first time.

Safi looked up and growled. Mandy tensed up. Had Simba moved in too early, before the cub had finished with the meat? Was he warning them off?

But the boy stayed calm. 'It's his call,' he told her. 'He's saying "*Jambo*"!'

She relaxed. And now the cub began to purr as Simba approached him. Leaving the remains of his food, Safi trotted to meet him. Soon the boy and the cub were stroking and nuzzling, making their soft greeting sounds.

'Come over here!' Simba called for Mandy and James. 'Safi wants to meet his new friends.'

They eased forward. At any moment Safi might take fright. But Simba murmured gently and stroked him all the while. The lonely cub nuzzled up to him and purred.

'You can touch him,' he said, seeing that Mandy hesitated.

She reached out to stroke Safi's soft, warm fur. He turned his head to look at her.

'He says "*Karibu*". Welcome,' Simba whispered.

Mandy sighed and smiled, then gave way to James. She watched the two of them make friends. 'How come he's so tame?' she asked Simba.

'He's not tame. He's still free and wild. But he trusts you.'

For the first time Mandy noticed the boy's smile. It spread slowly across his whole face, showing his white teeth, lighting up his eyes. 'You mean he trusts *you*!' she said, smiling back.

They set off at nine o'clock on the first day of their trek north to the Mountains of the Moon.

Simba led the way, sure-footed and silent, with Safi trotting close behind. Mandy and James found they had to work hard to keep up as they strode along the shore. Soon their legs ached and they grew short of breath.

But Mandy refused to admit she was tired. 'We're Safi's new pride!' she told James. 'It looks like he's definitely decided to adopt us!'

James wiped his forehead. 'He was probably fed up with being by himself. He's missing his family, so he has to make do with us instead.'

'Yes, and he knows where his next meal is coming from!' Mandy knew enough about animals to realise that the way to their hearts was usually through their stomachs.

'It's more than that though.' James had admired Simba's way with the cub. 'I think it really is to do with trust.'

Mandy hitched her rucksack up her back and walked on. Safi had stopped to stare at two large brown ducks who swam dangerously close to the water's edge. She wondered just how much the cub understood. 'Do you suppose he knows where we're taking him?'

'And why?'

'Yes. I mean, has he got any sense of direction, for instance? Would he know that his mother had been taken to the Ruwenzori Park?' She stopped to wait for the cub.

'Would he?' James looked ahead to ask the expert.

Simba retraced his steps. 'Yes. You saw him call across the lake for her to come. He knows.' Glancing up at the sun, then at their two hot faces, he decided it was time to rest.

'No, we can go on if you like,' Mandy insisted. 'You don't need to stop just for us.'

'It's midday. We'll stop for the cub.'

Simba called to Safi in Swahili, moving away from the water to a cool place under the trees.

They sat in a small group, grateful for the shade.

'Is he hungry?' James asked, pointing at Safi.

Simba sat cross-legged on the ground. He looked across the water at the still distant mountains, thinking faraway thoughts. 'No.'

'Thirsty?' Mandy wondered.

'Yes.'

She took her bottle and poured fresh water into her palm. Stretching out her hand, she offered it to the cub. Safi sniffed at it then lapped eagerly.

'Good.' Simba nodded without looking at her.

Pleased with his praise, she screwed the cap tight and began to stroke Safi's soft head.

'You're not afraid?' Simba said quietly, still looking into the distance.

'Of Safi? No, of course not.' Mandy was frightened of some things; of fast cars, heights, of men with guns. But she loved all animals.

Simba was silent. They were surrounded by the hum of insects, the dry rustle of grass, the lapping of the water on the shore.

James was the one who remembered their promise to call Kampi ya Simba on the radio. He took it out of his rucksack and his voice cut into the peace and quiet.

'We're fine,' he told Adam Hope on the receiving end of their signal. 'We've come a long way.' They'd walked for three hours without a break. 'I think it must be about fifteen kilometres.'

'That's great. Is it hard work?'

'Yep. It's pretty hot right now, so we stopped to rest.'

'Good. And how's the cub?'

'Great. Simba soon tracked him down, and now he's made best friends with Mandy!' He grinned as Mandy blushed. 'She's sitting here stroking him like mad. You should see her!'

'I wish I could.' Mr Hope's voice crackled and faded. 'Listen, James, thanks for checking in with us. Get in touch again before dark.'

James promised they would, then switched off the radio. Then, dipping into his bag he drew out a squashed, flat shape. 'Hey, we'd better eat this chocolate before it melts completely!' he told them.

Mandy noticed Simba sniff as James unwrapped the chocolate and broke it into pieces. He pretended to ignore them, still sitting with his back half-turned.

'Here, have some.' James nudged him in the back.

Sulkily the Masai boy shook his head.

'Yes, it's OK; look!' James popped some into his own mouth. 'Chocolate. Lovely and sweet. It's gone, see!'

Simba grunted.

'Take a bit.'

Slowly the boy took the chocolate. He watched it melt against his warm fingers, put it to his nose, smelled it warily. Then he decided it was safe to try it. James and Mandy watched his eyes open wide at the taste.

'Is it good?' James asked.

Simba nodded as he licked his fingers clean. 'Chocolate!'

So they shared the whole bar while Safi sat happily beside them, his head resting on his paws. Then they drank water, waited for the heat to die down, watched the animals come slowly to the lake to drink.

'Hippos,' Simba said quietly.

They studied the surface of the lake. Insects droned on. Safi was asleep with his head on Mandy's lap. 'I can't see anything,' James complained.

Mandy too saw nothing unusual. Then she looked harder. What seemed to be smooth grey rocks at the edge of the lake had begun to move. Mud churned up, water swirled, and then a hippo opened its huge pink mouth and yawned.

For Mandy, it was another marvel of nature, something she'd only ever seen in the animal books that lined her shelves back home in Welford.

More of the great beasts snorted and came up for air. They jostled one another and turned slowly, the wet mud glistening on their broad grey backs. She shook her head. 'I can't believe it; real live hippopotamuses!'

'Hippopotam*i*,' James said under his breath.

'You mustn't go near,' Simba warned.

'Why not? They're not dangerous, are they?' Mandy thought they were slow and funny. How could they do any harm?

'Yes. And buffalo and baboon and elephant. Even monkeys can harm you.' Simba reeled off a list.

'And lions?' she teased, tickling Safi's soft ear as he slept.

'Yes, of course, lions,' he said seriously and stood up. 'Remember this.'

'But not if they trust you,' Mandy objected. 'Isn't that what you told us?'

Simba shook his head. 'The lion is strong and

fast. He's the most dangerous of all.'

They took his word for it and prepared to set off once more. Even so, Mandy felt she was floating on air as they continued on their way. Soon the grass grew high and more lush, the trees thickened. The landscape was changing; there was more shade, but the going was harder.

But they tramped on, following in Simba's footsteps, to Zebra Camp, where they would spend their first night in the bush. And with Safi trotting at her side, skipping off every now and then to explore a stream or to chase after a tempting sound from a nearby bush, Mandy knew she could have walked for ever.

Eight

'Where should this peg go?' Mandy took the last one from her tent bag. Setting up a tent in semi-darkness wasn't easy. She frowned and scratched her head, squinting through the dusk at the botched job she'd made of it. The walls sagged and flapped in the breeze, and she saw now that the whole thing was on a slant.

James took the peg from her and shoved it in the ground. He hooked a guy-rope under it. 'You just tighten it like this and the tent straightens up!' His own tent was pitched perfectly. 'It's a good job it's not going to rain,' he said. 'I don't think you'd stay dry if it did!'

'So? No problem. *Hakuna matata*!' She didn't

care about the tent. They'd arrived at Zebra
Camp and Charles Tawana had given them a
warm welcome. Then, at six o'clock, Mandy had
radioed her mum and dad. Safi had been fed,
settled down close to Simba, and afterwards
they'd sat down by the fire to a meal of bread,
eggs and vegetables. 'All I want to do now is
sleep!' she yawned.

'Me too.' James unrolled his sleeping bag.

'What about you, Simba?' Mandy caught sight
of him standing a few metres away, looking out
at the lake. Safi still sat quietly at his feet. 'Where
will you sleep?'

'Here.' He'd chosen a spot sheltered by trees
but clear of the tents.

'With Safi?' She felt guilty that he had no tent
or sleeping bag to keep out the cold mist which
would roll down from the mountains. So she
took her own bag over to him. 'Use this. It'll
keep you warm.'

He looked curiously at it, felt its padded
surface, examined its long silver zip. He grinned
then shook his head. Instead he gathered up
his long red robe and wrapped it round his
shoulders like a blanket.

'Is that all you've got?'

Simba smiled but didn't answer. He began to

explain the route for the next day. 'I want to finish the journey by tomorrow night, to give ourselves the third day to find the cub's pride. We'll walk for three, maybe four hours after dawn. Then, when we reach the place where the hills meet the water, we'll rest.'

'Then walk some more?' She could see in the moonlight that the Ruwenzori Mountains were still a long way off.

He nodded.

'Don't you ever get tired, Simba?'

'Sometimes.'

Mandy wondered if his legs ached as much as hers did. 'And will you be able to sleep in the cold?'

'Safi will keep me warm.'

She looked down at the cub. He had his head up, listening to the sounds of the bush. Suddenly a new thought struck her. 'He won't go wandering off, will he?' She knew lions roamed and hunted for food at night.

'Maybe.'

She was startled. 'What if he gets lost?'

Simba smiled. 'I'll call him back.'

'And what if something attacks him? A hyena or a jackal?' She caught a faint howl from across the wide plain. She imagined eyes glittering and shadowy shapes prowling towards them.

'I'll be there to help.'

'So you won't be sleeping?' This didn't seem fair; why should James and she sleep while Simba kept watch? 'We could help,' she suggested shyly.

So they arranged a rota of sleeping and watching. Simba would guard Safi for two hours while James and Mandy slept. Then Mandy would take over, then James, and so on. This way Simba would feel rested for the day ahead too.

'If there's trouble, wake me,' he told Mandy when she went to take his place by the sleeping cub at eleven o'clock.

She nodded and shivered in the night air.

'Watch and listen,' he warned. 'You know the sound of hyena?'

Again she nodded. With chattering teeth she stared into the black shadows.

Satisfied, Simba took a last look at Safi. 'The cub's tired. He's fed well. There will be no need for him to hunt.'

Then he went a few metres off, wrapped his cloak round him and lay on the ground. Soon he was fast asleep.

Mandy kept watch for two quiet hours. She

sat under the stars listening to the leaves rustle, the creak and groan of branches overhead, the far-off call of jackals. Through it all Safi slept trustingly, head tucked between his big round paws.

Next morning they had broken camp and were ready to leave before daybreak. Charles made them drink hot tea and eat toast. He told them that the latest radio signals still showed that the Lake Kasanka lions were settling well in their new mountain home.

'The first pride, the white group, has marked out a territory here.' He drew them into his office and pointed to a map similar to the one Levina had shown them. 'This covers twenty square kilometres.' Charles was excited to share what he knew. He was a young student, proud to work on the project with Dr Lemiso, he told them. 'Pride number two, the red one, has settled here in a smaller area. And pride number three, the blue, is higher up the mountain, here.'

'How high is that?' James asked.

'Two thousand metres.'

'That's high!' he whistled. Then a new thought struck him. 'How will we know which pride Safi belongs to?' he asked Simba.

The boy shrugged. '*They'll* know.'

'Who? The lions?'

'Yes.' Simba showed his impatience to set off by his short, abrupt answer. He glanced at the sun rising above the rim of the crater.

So Mandy and James thanked Charles and heaved their rucksacks on to their backs. They set off, walking at a steady pace, heading north, still following the shoreline. As before, Simba led the way.

Mandy was happy to be on the move. As yet the day was cool and fresh, and Safi trotted quietly at her side. She had time to think ahead to how it would be when they finally reached the national park. She could hardly wait to see Safi reunited with his mother. 'I think he knows where we're going,' she murmured to James. Safi seemed eager this morning, intent on keeping up with them instead of going off on side-tracks to play or hunt.

'I don't see how we can prove it.' James was as logical as ever.

'They say animals sense these things,' she insisted. 'You know those stories about cats and dogs getting lost and walking hundreds of miles to find their owners.'

He raised his eyebrows. 'Maybe.'

'Definitely.' Mandy hummed brightly as they walked on. To the west of them a large herd of zebra grazed.

They went on until Simba spotted buffalo ahead. He signalled for them to stop.

'What's wrong? Won't they just ignore us?' James cast an uneasy eye at the big horns of the male buffaloes. The creatures were wide at the shoulder and slim at the hips; several hundred kilos of solid muscle and bone.

Simba shook his head. 'They'll attack if we go on. They have young ones to protect.'

Mandy saw small calves close to their mothers. The big males gathered, ready to charge. She crouched to put an arm around Safi's neck and hold him back. 'What do we do now? Wait until they decide to move off?'

'No.' Simba decided they should make a wide detour. He led them away from the lake and the buffaloes, into the trees that fringed this part of the plain. The animals watched them go, then settled calmly to graze once more.

But the extra distance had delayed them. It took a full hour of struggling through thick bushes and trees before they could return to their original track. Now, with the danger safely behind them, James paused to look at his watch.

'I vote we stop for a bit,' he said.

Reluctantly, Simba agreed.

'Just for half an hour.' Mandy flopped to the ground.

'You two rest,' Simba told them.

So they unscrewed their water-bottles and drank. When they looked again, Simba had vanished.

'Safi, stay here!' Mandy whispered. The cub had got to his feet, ready to go off and find the boy. 'That's a good boy. Simba will soon be back!'

'We hope!' James searched the scene in vain. 'I wish he wouldn't keep on vanishing for no good reason.'

'You wait; there's bound to be a reason,' Mandy insisted.

And, sure enough, when Simba came back, he carried fresh meat. He threw it down without a word and the hungry cub seized it.

'See!' Mandy whispered. But she didn't feel brave enough to ask questions. She was happier not knowing what Simba had hunted and how.

As soon as the cub had finished, Simba said they should move on. He seemed edgy, and if anything more silent than before.

'We have to use the radio first,' Mandy

reminded them. 'Mum and Dad will be waiting to hear from us.'

They soon made contact and caught up with the news. Joseph and Levina were back from Arusha, Emily Hope told them. Matthew Mulakesi and his wardens were still a hundred kilometres to the north, chasing off the elephant poachers.

'Well, we're all fine here,' Mandy told her, speaking clearly into the microphone. 'We've been walking all morning and we're ahead of schedule. Safi has just been fed.'

'So everything's going according to plan?'

'Except for a detour around some angry buffaloes, yes. I'd better go now, though. Simba's waiting. We'll get in touch again tonight. OK?'

Mandy packed up the radio in a hurry. Safi seemed to have picked up Simba's impatience. The two of them stood by the lake, almost straining to be on their way, she thought. And when they set off, their pace was faster than before.

'It looks like he's making up for lost time,' James decided. They were almost running to keep up.

'Or else he saw something he didn't like when

he was out hunting.' Mandy paused mid-stride. 'You don't think that could be it?'

'Don't ask me.' They fell silent, concentrating on the way ahead.

They'd plunged into an area of wet marshland close to the edge of the lake, their feet sinking into the soft earth. Mandy looked up again. She saw Safi vanishing amongst some tall reeds. 'Hey, come back!' she called. 'He'll get lost if he's not careful,' she muttered, staggering on through the swamp.

A few metres ahead, Simba stopped.

'Where's Safi? I can't see him!' she yelled.

He looked hard, then pointed. 'There.'

Mandy heard a splash and saw the cub leap out of the wet marsh towards the shallow waves at the edge of the lake. He landed up to his belly, coughed and swallowed water. Then he reared up and leaped on, in and out of the reeds.

'Come back!' Mandy insisted. She was worried that he would find himself out of his depth. 'I'm going after him!' she told the others.

But Simba darted towards her and held her back. Without saying a word he pointed at the rocks where she was about to tread.

They started to shift. Mud sucked and oozed as the 'rocks' rose from the water.

'More hippos!' James cried.

Mandy gasped. Seconds later, and she would have landed amongst them.

By this time Safi had managed to splash to safety on the far side of the marsh. His feet were back on firm ground. But the hippos were angry at the disturbance. They opened their wide mouths; four, five, six of them altogether, standing between Mandy and the cub. Simba grabbed her by the arm and pulled her back.

'Safi is scared!' she protested. He was soaked through and leaping off across dry land, gathering speed as he ran away from the hippos.

The boy insisted that she couldn't follow him. 'Wait.' He took her back to James and together they retreated the way they'd come.

'We've lost him. He's out of sight!' Mandy's legs were scratched, her clothes dripping wet. By now Safi had reached the cover of some rocks.

'It's OK, Mandy, he'll come back,' James told her. 'Once he gets over his shock he'll come looking for us.'

Simba agreed. He watched the hippos swirl through the mud, plodding slowly away. They'd lost interest in the intruders and were heading for clear water.

'Shouldn't we follow him?' Mandy fixed her gaze on the odd-shaped rock where she'd last seen the cub. It rose like a giant loaf from the sloping hillside.

'What if he comes back and we're not here?' James pointed out. 'Listen; I'll stay. You go with Simba.'

They agreed the plan. 'Don't move! Pray that he comes back!' Mandy hissed. It was all she had time to say before Simba began to move off towards the rock.

She felt the heat soak into her as they ran. It sapped her energy so that her feet dragged across the dry earth. She stumbled, then pulled herself upright. All the time Simba was increasing the distance between them, his swift legs speeding ahead. When Mandy finally reached the rock, he'd already scrambled up its face and was peering up the slope beyond.

'Can you see him?' Mandy's fingers searched for hand-holds in the rock. Breathlessly, she pulled herself up to join him. The scene swam dizzily ahead of her; a long stretch of open country, wave after wave of unbroken savanna. There was no sign of the cub amongst the rippling grass. 'He could be anywhere!' How could they see one small cub amidst this vast sea of pale gold?

But Simba seemed to be pointing to a place beyond the grassland. His gaze was fixed on a distant trail of dust that drew gradually nearer.

Mandy saw it with a puzzled frown, slow to realise what it might be. But then she made out the three jeeps heading towards them; still tiny in the distance, kicking up the familiar trail. What could it mean?

Simba looked at them through narrow, unblinking eyes, his mouth curled in disgust.

'Is it Southall?' Mandy cried with a sinking heart.

The boy nodded but said nothing.

'Did you know they were coming?'

'I heard their cars earlier,' he admitted, 'when I went hunting for meat.'

They were the same jeeps as before; three cars loaded with men with licences and guns. 'But he promised!' Mandy's voice fell to a whisper. 'He was supposed to give us three days!'

Simba stared stubbornly at the tell-tale cloud.

'He's broken his promise!' Still she refused to believe it. Safi was out there, scared and lost, and now they had to stand helpless as the farmers drove on to the slope.

A loud, sharp shot rang through the air. It was true; the hunters were back!

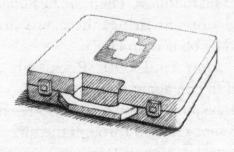

Nine

The animals on the Lake Kasanka plain reared up and fled in panic. Gazelles scattered as shots echoed from the guns. Flamingos beat their loud wings, rose up from the lake and flew away. In every corner, beneath every bush, small creatures froze in terror.

Mandy kept on repeating the broken promise. 'Three days!' She'd been there, heard it with her own ears. 'It's not fair!' Stranded on the rock, they watched helplessly.

'Come on, what are we waiting for?' James had come running up from the lake at the sound of the guns. He stopped beside the rock, but he was ready to go on into the path of the jeeps.

She got set to follow. Then she hesitated. The men had stopped firing; there was an eerie silence. 'Maybe it's too late!'

'We'll soon find out!' Recklessly James prepared to run again.

But Simba jumped down and stood in his way. Another shot cracked through the air.

'What are you doing? Don't you want to save Safi?' Mandy cried. She too jumped down and tried to dodge past him, but Simba stood firm.

'Guns!' he warned.

'We know they've got guns! That's why we have to stop them!' In her panic, Mandy had lost all her common sense.

'How? What can we do against guns?' He reminded her what her parents had said. 'No, we have to stay here.'

She stared at him, torn by her urge to help Safi and the promises she'd made to her mother and father. 'We've got to do something!' she pleaded. 'How can we make them stop firing?'

It seemed hopeless. They stood face to face, neither Mandy nor Simba ready to give way. Meanwhile, the guns fell silent and the jeeps continued their search.

'If we can't go to him, call him back here!'

Mandy urged. 'You can do it, Simba; make Safi come back to us!'

'I can try.' He agreed to climb back on to the rock. He stood on the smooth summit and cupped his hands around his mouth. He called out, waited, called again.

Nothing happened. Dozens of small deer scattered as the jeeps ploughed on through the grass. There were more frightened cries, birds flew up and wheeled overhead.

'Safi!' Mandy scrambled up beside Simba. 'Here we are! Come back this way!' Her voice got lost in the empty air.

But as she called, the jeeps slowed and changed direction. James saw them turn and head for their rock. 'They've seen us!' he warned.

Mandy waited, trembling from head to foot. She felt Simba freeze beside her, his hatred for the men coming through loud and clear in his fierce eyes and deep scowl. 'If they've killed Safi . . . !' The words died in her throat.

The nightmare vehicles cut through the long grass towards them. They could make out the figures inside, the raised shotguns. Southall drove ahead of the others, cutting carelessly through a herd of terrified impala. When he drew within shouting distance of the rock, he braked suddenly. The door opened and he strode across.

'Get out of here!' He waved his arms at them. 'Go on, clear off!' It was plain that he didn't intend to spend time arguing.

'We're not going anywhere.' Mandy found her voice. They had right on their side. Anyway, for as long as they stood there within range of the men's guns, Safi would be safe. Even Southall would have to hold his fire.

'I'm warning you!' He stared up at them, his face red, his jaw clenched.

'You gave us three days.' She wouldn't back down. She would stay until they came and carried her down from the rock. Simba and James would stick with her, she knew.

'More fool me!' he said bitterly. 'I give you time and look what happens. One of my calves gets mauled and killed, that's what!'

'When?' Mandy shot back at him suspiciously.

'Last night. That cub crept in right under our noses. First thing this morning we find the calf dead!'

'That's not possible!' James protested. He tried to get Southall to listen to reason. 'It can't have been Safi; he was with us at Zebra Camp!'

'Says you!' the farm manager retorted. He didn't like being argued with. 'Why should I believe that? This attack had lion-cub written all over it. The calf was badly mauled, but not killed outright. Whatever it was went for the neck.'

Mandy shuddered. 'But it wasn't Safi!' she insisted. They'd kept watch; the cub had slept all through the night.

'Look, I don't have time to waste. I'm warning you; I'm going back now and I'm going to give the order for the hunt to go on. If you don't get out of the way, that's up to you. I've given you fair warning!'

Mandy made one last attempt to convince him. 'Mr Southall, it could have been a hyena, a jackal, anything! It wasn't our cub, honestly!' She wanted to plead for more time.

But he turned his back and strode off. The other men sat watching. This time there would be no deals, no promises. As far as they were concerned Safi was guilty. And now they were out to get the lion that had killed their calf.

As the jeeps curved away across the hill, Mandy sagged against the rock. What now? Simba had climbed back to call for Safi again, but the alarm among the animals had spread far and wide. His voice didn't rise above the galloping hooves which crashed through the bushes away from the engines' roar.

'Let's try the lake,' she said to James. Simba could stay and call while they ran back to the spot where the cub had last seen them. 'Maybe he'll try to get back there!'

So they sprinted down the hill. With every step Mandy dreaded the sound of fresh gunfire. When it came, shattering the air once more, she willed herself to go on.

At last they reached the marshy ground that had separated them from their cub. They ran into a silent, empty scene; no sign of the hippos, nothing. James shook his head hopelessly. 'Safi must have been too scared of the guns to make his way back.'

But Mandy still hoped. She had faith in the cub. 'He's clever,' she reminded James. 'If he had come back, he wouldn't just stand around and wait. He'd take cover.'

So they stayed to look for him; quietly at first, then Mandy began to call his name. 'Safi!' She called softly, then crept on, longing for an answering growl.

When at last he limped from the cover of

some bushes at the water's edge, she could have cried with relief. Weary and scared, he'd heard her voice and came whimpering towards her.

'He's hurt!' James said. 'There's something the matter with his front paw.'

They watched as he took slow, painful steps towards them.

'It's not serious, is it?' James said. 'It couldn't be a gunshot wound, could it?'

Mandy bent down and held out her hand. Safi came to her and sank to the ground. She stroked him gently. His sides heaved, he whimpered with exhaustion. 'I don't think so. I can't see any blood,' she whispered. She didn't want to hurt the injured paw, or to upset him, so she waited until Safi grew calm.

'I'll get the first-aid kit out.' Quickly James unstrapped his rucksack and took out the blue plastic box.

'There, there.' Mandy soothed Safi. He blinked up at her as he lay on his side, the injured paw stretched straight out. 'Let me see.' She stroked the paw and gently turned it so that she could see the soft pads underneath.

Safi growled and lifted his head.

'Careful!' James hovered behind her.

'It's OK, I'll try not to hurt you.' She leaned

forward to inspect the wound. 'He's picked up something sharp, look. In between his toes.' There it was; a long thorn digging into the softest part of his foot. 'I need a pair of tweezers to get it out.'

James searched the box. 'We haven't got any tweezers. Will these do?' He handed her a small pair of scissors, used for cutting bandages.

She shrugged. 'I'll try. Now, Safi, you have to stay still.' She talked softly as she worked at the wound. 'The thing is, this might hurt a bit. But once I get it out, you'll feel fine.'

The cub stared into her face, listening quietly. He only growled when the points of the scissors touched the thorn.

'It's in quite deep,' Mandy told James. She opened the scissors a fraction and with a steady hand she took hold of the painful thorn. 'Got it!'

Safi growled again, but he didn't move.

'That's it, good boy!' Mandy took care not to snip through the brittle spike and leave part of it in the sore flesh. She pulled gently. Slowly, bit by bit, she eased it free.

She held it in the air to show James and they both breathed a sigh of relief. The thorn was at least three centimetres long.

'Now we need antiseptic cream,' Mandy said, stroking Safi's neck. Seeming to realise that she'd done the trick, he purred softly as she dabbed the cream between his toes.

'Great.' James stood back and admired the work. 'You'll make a good vet, Mandy.'

She blushed. 'We'd better go and tell Simba that we've found Safi,' she reminded him.

'Without letting Southall and the rest know. If they find out, they'll be straight after us.' James packed away the first-aid kit. 'Do you think Safi is fit to carry on?'

Mandy nodded. 'I hope so. We have to get out of here as quickly as we can.'

So James ran quietly up the slope to Simba's rock. He told him the good news and the two boys ran back together. By the time they reached the shore, Mandy had got Safi back on his feet.

He looked up at the sound of running feet.

Simba's bright red robe flew back in the breeze; his long legs strode down the hill. He smiled and laughed as he reached the cub, then he dropped to his knees and held him tight.

Mandy grinned at James. 'Ready?' she asked Simba softly.

The sun was at its highest, the heat beat down. But the whine of jeeps in the distance spurred them on. The Masai boy glanced at the cub standing shakily beside him. 'OK, we go on,' he said.

had happened. Perhaps he would drive out and try to persuade Southall to keep the bargain he'd made with her dad.

'Any luck?' James strained to hear a reply over the crackle and hiss of the radio transmitter.

She shook her head. 'Maybe they're all out working in the crater somewhere.' It was three o'clock. Intense heat rose from the baked earth. Quietly she packed up the radio and got ready to go on.

But Simba signalled for her to wait. He'd climbed the tree for a better view of the jeeps, and now he called softly from a low branch. 'They're coming this way!'

So Mandy sat with Safi, stroking and soothing him while the dreaded engine noise drew near. The cub could sense the fear behind her soft words. She felt him grow tense. 'It's OK, Safi, we'll look after you!' She put her arms round his neck, hearing a deep rumble in his throat.

The jeeps came nearer still. Hidden in his branch, Simba crouched like a lion ready to drop and pounce. Below him, in the shade of the huge trunk, Mandy and James could see only dust, hear only the rising roar of the engines.

'It's a good job we weren't out in the open,' James whispered.

'We were lucky.' She felt Safi shuffle restlessly. 'It's OK, we won't let them harm you,' she told him again.

The farmers came close to the lake, twisting and winding through the bushes, their jeeps throwing up red dust and crunching over the rough ground. Once they stopped to take a good look by the water's edge. The three engines died. There was silence.

'Shh!' Mandy urged. Safi had got up on to his feet, every nerve attuned to the presence of the men. He growled out a warning.

Seconds ticked by. Mandy crouched behind the giant tree, one arm round the cub. She prayed that Safi wouldn't attract attention.

A careless impala wandered out of the nearby scrub, just metres away, busy nibbling at the juicy grass. 'Oh no!' James whispered. 'If Safi sees him, he's bound to try and hunt him!'

But luckily the men in the jeep saw the deer first. Mandy heard Southall point it out and then shout an order to move on. As the engines coughed into life, the impala took fright. Soon a cloud of dust showed that the men had driven on.

Simba dropped silently from the tree, his face tense.

'What happened? Why did they decide to go?' James asked.

'The impala helped us,' he explained. 'The men saw him and thought there could be no lion near here.'

'Because the deer would have spotted Safi and run away long ago!' James realised.

'Well done, Safi!' Mandy stroked and petted him. 'You didn't give us away!' He purred and rolled on to his side.

'How far now?' James grew practical. He had his rucksack on his back, and was staring in the direction of the mountains.

'Two hours, maybe more,' Simba said.

'That means we can still get there before dark.' Mandy was ready to move on. 'Let's go before that lot decide to turn back this way!' Despite the delays, and despite Southall's betrayal, she felt now that they were going to make it.

But it was a tiring trek. They plodded through reeds and marshes, through bone-dry dust and craggy rocks, through spiky bushes, across dangerous stretches of open sand. With each change in the landscape there was a fresh challenge, and by late afternoon Mandy ached from head to foot.

'We're nearly there!' she promised a weary Safi. The Ruwenzori Mountains loomed large at the end of the lake. Shadows lay deep in the valleys, though the peaks were still golden in the sun.

The cub padded on obediently.

And at last, after two long days, they left the shores of Lake Kasanka behind. They began the trudge out of the crater up a gradual slope towards the mountains. Using the cover of trees and bushes, they managed to keep out of sight of the men in their jeeps.

'Phew, thank heavens!' James gathered the energy to break the weary silence. Though the three cars still zig-zagged across the flat basin of land below them, they were by now a long way off. 'We made it!'

'Are you sure?' Mandy raised her head. She'd been plodding on, making sure that Safi stayed close by her side. 'Won't there be a fence?'

'What fence?'

'Around the Ruwenzori National Park.' She'd pictured a gate, a proper boundary.

'It doesn't look like there is one. Let's ask Simba.'

From up ahead the boy heard his name. He stopped and waited.

'Are we in the park?' she asked him.

'Almost.'

She glanced back at the tiny jeeps scouring the valley for their cub. 'How will we know?'

'When we reach the thorntrees.' He pointed to a row of the familiar tall trees growing along a low ridge in the shadow of the mountains. 'All the land after that is safe for the cub.'

She nodded and gathered her last ounce of strength to cover the ground.

'We beat them after all!' James breathed. He gritted his teeth and tramped up the hill.

'They won't get you now!' Mandy promised. Safi limped beside her, head up, as if he knew the end of the journey was near.

Simba walked on ahead; a tall, straight figure, looking up at the mountains. He was still alert, as at last they reached the dark row of thorns.

'This is it. This is your new home!' Mandy looked around. It was good lion country, according to Simba. There was a wide sweep of open grassland that led to the mountains, scattered with trees and rocks; good hiding places for lions and other predators.

And the park was teeming with wildlife. Mandy could see a family of giraffes under a tree, reaching up to feed. And there were deer of all kinds; topi, impala, gazelles. Simba named them all.

'What about elephants?' James seemed to have forgotten how tired he was. He strode here and there, wanting to see everything all at once.

Simba nodded. 'Many.'

'Where?'

'Far to the north, following the rains.'

'Won't we see them?'

'Not today.'

'Never mind,' Mandy said. 'We still have to find Safi's pride before dark.' Their rescue wouldn't be over until the cub was back with his own family.

'Well, we must be close.' He turned to Simba. 'This is roundabout the place where Levina and Charles tracked the white pride. It was just over the boundary to the park.'

But the Masai boy didn't need maps and tags. 'I've seen lion prints,' he said quietly.

'Why didn't you tell us?' Forgetting how tired she was, Mandy was ready to spring into action. There was no time to lose.

'Be careful!' Ignoring their excitement, Simba began to pick up other signs that the lions were nearby. Then he checked the direction of the wind, the lengthening shadows. At last he decided which way to go.

They stole after him, through the thorntrees towards a rocky ridge. There, basking in the last patch of warm sunlight, they saw their first pride of lions.

Three lionesses lay in the golden light, the nearest one stretched out on her side to feed two cubs. The little ones were smaller than Safi, still tiny balls of pale fluff. They were tucked close to their mother, feeding happily. A second lioness sat and groomed a larger cub. She licked him and scratched him gently with her big paws. The cub licked her in return and tumbled over her. Then there was a third female sitting alone, her great head raised and gazing down into the valley.

Mandy felt her heart jump. They had crouched down behind a rock to view the pride in secret, but now Safi seemed to have scented them. His ears were up, his eyes glowing in the shadows.

'Is that his mother?' Mandy pointed to the lonely female. She hoped it might be, yet she found herself ready to cry at the idea of having to say goodbye to Safi.

'Wait.' Simba made sure that the lioness still

hadn't spotted them. 'Here comes the big one; the male.'

His words sent a thrill through her. She felt the hairs at the back of her neck rise and prickle. Every shadow seemed to hold a mystery. Mandy peered in all directions, waiting for the lion to appear.

He came stalking across the ridge; a huge, powerful male. His tail swung behind him, his long back swayed as he walked.

James and Mandy stared spellbound from behind the rock, while Simba held tight to Safi.

The lion paused, then strode on behind more rocks. They caught glimpses of him; his strong legs, the whisk of his tail. Then he appeared again, curving round the solitary female, head raised, staring in their direction.

He was a magnificent lion. His head was huge, his mane thick and black.

When he opened his mouth to roar, Mandy felt the noise shake her whole body. But the moment she saw his wonderful head, she knew this wasn't the leader of Safi's pride. Simba had told them that Safi's father had a golden mane; this one's was pure black. Now that she dared to take a second look, she saw that the lion had

leaped to the highest rock, where he prowled to and fro.

What would he do next? Had he seen them? Mandy glanced at Simba, who had his finger raised to his mouth, ordering silence.

Still trembling, Mandy ducked her head and closed her eyes. Again the lion's roar split the evening air. It rumbled down the valley and echoed through the mountains, telling everyone that this was his land.

Then it stopped as suddenly as it had started. The silence was almost more terrifying still. Where was he now? What was he up to? Mandy looked up. The rock was deserted.

Mandy and James stared at the spot where the pride of lions had been. They gasped and turned to Simba. The boy kept his finger to his mouth. At last, after several minutes, he nodded.

'Where did they go?' James breathed.

'Down to the water,' the boy told them. He explained that the lion's roar was only a warning. 'He was letting us know that this is his new home.'

'Did he know we were here?'

Simba nodded. 'He didn't see us, but he smelled us and heard us.'

'Would he have attacked?' Mandy was just beginning to recover.

'No.' Simba stood up. In the dusk light, his red cloak looked almost black. 'He knows we're his friends.'

'I wouldn't have liked to test it out,' James joked nervously. He was dusting himself down, wiping his glasses with shaking hands. 'What now?'

'We can walk for twenty, maybe thirty minutes more,' Simba told them. 'Then it will be dark.'

Mandy glanced around. They hadn't been planning to spend another night in the bush. Now, whether or not they found Safi's family before nightfall, it looked like this was what they would have to do. She could see the lake shining silver a long way below, and the mountains casting their purple shadow above. 'We've got two prides to choose from,' she reminded them. 'Which way should we try first?'

It was James's methodical thinking that helped them make the decision. 'Think about it; this is the white pride, with four adult lions. Levina and Charles tagged them and tracked them on the map, remember. The red pride is over to the east. But that only has three adults together. The blue pride went higher up the mountain. There were six pins for them. So, if it's the biggest pride, there's more chance that they have more cubs there, and that makes it more likely that the wardens would make a mistake and leave one behind in the first place!'

Mandy worked it out and agreed. 'But that means we should try further up the mountain, worse luck.' It meant another steep climb ahead.

'Yes, and we'll definitely have to camp out, so we'll have to radio your mum and dad.'

'OK?' Mandy checked with Simba that this was the best plan. She needn't have asked. He'd listened to James and agreed. Already he was setting off up the hillside.

So they trekked on into the dusk. For a few

minutes the sun hung over the horizon, a golden-red ball of fire. Mandy glanced down at Safi. Ever since she'd taken the thorn from his foot, he'd stuck close to her side. Now he padded softly up the mountain, almost at their journey's end.

The cub had taken to her and claimed her as if she were his own mother. But tonight or tomorrow they would find his true family and would leave her. Mandy sighed, then looked up as the sun sank behind the mountain and day turned to night.

Eleven

Mandy slept fitfully in the open air. Up here on the mountain there was no flat land to pitch the tents, and night had come suddenly and found them unprepared. Inside her sleeping bag, staring up at the stars, Mandy heard the stiff breeze rustle through the grass.

Every noise seemed to keep her awake; the whistling wind, the small rattles and scratchings of animals busy with their night-time search for food. As she listened, she found she missed the gentle lapping of the waves on the shore. Here, on the Mountains of the Moon, all was wild and strange.

Once more they'd agreed to take it in turns to watch over Safi.

'We don't want him to wander off into these other lions' territory,' James had said. 'Not until we find out for sure which pride he belongs to.' He'd volunteered to take the first watch while the others tried to rest.

But when Mandy found that she couldn't sleep, she crept out of her sleeping bag to join him and the cub. 'What have you seen?' she asked.

'Nothing.' James shook his head. 'It's so dark out there I can't see a blind thing!' He stared out across the wide, dark slopes, then up at the starry sky. 'There's a new moon, so it's giving off hardly any light,' he whispered.

Mandy shivered.

'Can't you sleep?' He sat with his sleeping bag round his shoulders, his knees hunched up against his chest.

'No. I keep thinking about tomorrow.'

'About saying goodbye?'

'Yep.'

He waited a while before he went on. 'You've done it before, Mandy; loads of times.' On all their rescue missions there was a point when it was time to return a wild animal to its natural home.

'I know. But this feels different somehow. This is a lion . . . a lion in Africa!' There were no words for how strongly she felt.

James sat quietly while Mandy went to fetch her own sleeping bag.

'Is it OK if I keep watch now?' she asked.

'It's not your turn yet. Why not try and get some sleep?'

Mandy shook her head. 'I can't. Anyway, you look tired. There's no point two people being awake.'

Gratefully he agreed and let her take over. It meant she would have extra time with Safi, watching him sleep soundly in his kitten position, head tucked between his paws, tail curled to keep himself warm.

Even when Simba came to take his turn in the middle of the night, she told him she still wasn't tired. Her eyes had grown used to the dark and she could pick him out, though his feet had made no sound in the grass. 'I'd rather stay here,' she insisted. The hours with Safi were slipping away.

Simba nodded and left her without a word. She stayed on watch, wide awake to the sound of every twig breaking underfoot in the nearby bushes, to scuffles, the snort of a warthog, the sharp, high cry of a startled bird. But then, as a dim grey light appeared in the east, Mandy's head began to nod. The sounds seemed to come from a long way off now, as if through a muffled screen. She lay down beside Safi and they fell silent. At last she slept.

When Mandy woke up, James was stooping over her, shaking her by the shoulder.

She jerked upright. 'Safi!' Her first thought was to make sure he was safe.

'It's OK, he's still asleep,' James whispered.

Mandy rubbed her eyes. The cub was curled in the same position, perfectly happy to sleep on. 'What time is it?'

'Just after six. Are you OK?'

'Yes, why?'

'Did you stay here all night?'

She nodded. 'When did this mist arrive?' The hills were covered in a thick white fog.

'I don't know; I just woke up and saw it. It's spooky!'

The mist cloaked the trees and spilled down towards the lake, making everything grey and ghostly. 'Where's Simba?' Mandy said suddenly.

'That's just it; I've no idea.' James was uneasy.

'That's why I thought I'd better wake you up. Did he say anything to you?'

'No. I wonder where he went.' Mandy couldn't see more than a few metres in front of her. 'James, have you got this sort of feeling . . .' she began.

' . . . that we're being watched?' James finished.

'Yes, Like there are eyes everywhere, even though we can't see them!' If James knew what she meant, surely the two of them couldn't both be mistaken.

'It could be hyenas,' James whispered. Wherever they went, they'd seen the stealthy creatures skulking in the bushes or speeding across the open plains.

'I wish Simba was here!'

'He's probably gone to fetch food for Safi.' James tried to pull himself together. 'I expect he'll be back any minute now.'

'Well, we'll have to keep guard anyway.' Swiftly she put her sleeping bag to one side. 'Listen; did you hear that?' It was the sound of an animal breathing hard after a long run; too close for comfort.

James nodded. 'Whatever it is, there's more than one of them!' There were noises all around, even a shadow or two lurking in the mist.

As soon as she was sure they were real, Mandy decided to wake the cub. He opened his eyes and grew alert on the instant.

'Shh!' she told him. 'Stay here!'

The animals in the fog grew bolder. She saw several creatures with big heads and blunt faces. They were yellowish-red, with sloping backs. As they slunk nearer, heads hanging, they opened their mouths to show yellow teeth.

'Definitely hyenas!' James whispered. 'What do we do now?'

'We stay put!' Mandy strained to see. 'Hyenas probably won't attack us.' There was a whole pack of them creeping round, panting and growling. Then one raised its head and gave a howling scream.

Safi reared up between them. He pawed the air, ready to fight.

More hyenas howled. Mandy and James looked round to grab stout sticks, stones; anything they could use to keep off the terrifying hunters.

Their black noses snuffled the air as they advanced. They surrounded Mandy and James as they stood firm to protect the cub.

'Who says they won't attack?' James breathed. He could see their spotted sides heaving as they moved in, their hot breath hanging in the cold morning air.

But then the excited howls began to die away. One hyena gave a different sound; a scream of anger. There was a low snarl from high up the slope. Half a dozen hyenas retreated, quick as a flash.

Now Safi crouched and whimpered. James's face was dead white as he looked out for this new creature that had scared off the hyenas. 'Does it sound like a lion to you?' he asked.

'Yes, and it's watching us. I can feel it.' Again Mandy felt her flesh begin to creep. *Hyenas were bad enough*, she thought.

Safi backed away, ready to turn and take flight. He whimpered loudly.

'No, it could be OK,' Mandy said out loud, sounding braver than she felt. 'If it *is* a lion up there, there's an even chance that it's one of Safi's own family!' They had to keep their nerve and find out. 'There's no point running away!'

James held his breath. The mist swirled and began to lift as the sun rose from behind the mountain ridge. 'Over there!' he said suddenly.

The lion stood beside a tall rock. He looked

down at them, his muzzle twisted into a snarl, his wide nose scarred from old battles, his yellow eyes gleaming. His mane was deep golden brown. It hung about his face and down his chest. It swung from side to side as the proud male strode down towards them.

Safi froze. Mandy saw his ears twitch, his whole body quiver.

Then a pale yellow lioness appeared from behind the rock. She followed the male down the hill; sleeker, slimmer, coming quickly for the cub. As she ran, she growled and called for Safi.

'It's your mother!' Mandy whispered. She dropped the stick she'd seized as a weapon and fell to her knees. 'She's come to find you!'

Safi hesitated and looked up at Mandy. His whimper grew louder.

'Here come two more cubs!' James said softly. They came tumbling and running down the hill after their mother.

Their own cub turned and purred. The male lion had stopped at a safe distance, but the mother and her cubs trotted on. At last, with a great leap of joy, Safi ran to meet them.

Mandy kneeled and watched the reunion. The mother lion bowed her head and let Safi cling to her neck. He fell and rolled on to the earth,

then was up and hurling himself at her again.
The other two cubs joined in. Soon there was a
rushing, tumbling bundle as three soft bodies
rolled down the hill towards James and Mandy.

She smiled through her tears as Safi broke
free and skipped up to them. He scrambled on
to her lap, inviting his brother and sister to meet
two of the humans who had saved his life. Soon
all three cubs wanted to play.

Mandy stroked them all. She smiled up at the
lioness who stood quietly watching. Then she
stood up and stepped back to join James.

As she let the cubs go, there was another
movement from further up the hill; a flash of
deep red, and then Simba stood beside the
proud male lion, head of the pride.

Slowly the lion turned his great head in
greeting. Simba spoke softly to him. They waited
as the lioness gathered the three cubs and
brought them up the hill. Then, when the whole
family was together once more, Simba broke
away and came silently down the slope.

'You went off to find Safi's pride, didn't you?'
James pressed Simba for an explanation. They
were packing their bags, ready to return to
the lake, where they had arranged to meet

their mum and dad in Levina's jeep.

The boy refused to answer. He stood grinning at Mandy's attempts to stuff her sleeping bag inside her rucksack.

'You did! That's why you left us alone with Safi!' James was all ready to leave. 'But you could have warned us!'

'You were asleep,' Simba said calmly.

'Anyway, I don't care,' Mandy sighed. 'All I care about is that Safi is safe with his family.' She was sad and happy; above all, proud of what they'd done.

The Masai boy nodded. He understood.

The warm sun had cleared the mist from the valley when they set off at last. Another day had begun, with no jeeps or guns to disturb the peace and quiet. Only the herds of gazelle and impala criss-crossed the valley, and as Mandy glanced back up the mountains, she could see a thin, pale moon fading in the morning sky.

'Goodbye, Safi,' she murmured.

Listening hard, she fancied she heard the roar of a young lion marking out his new territory high on the hill. She turned again and walked on with James and Simba, picturing their cub amongst the tall rocks and the wide seas of gently waving grass.

ANIMAL ARK

Lucy Daniels

1	KITTENS IN THE KITCHEN	£3.50	☐
2	PONY IN THE PORCH	£3.50	☐
3	PUPPIES IN THE PANTRY	£3.50	☐
4	GOAT IN THE GARDEN	£3.50	☐
5	HEDGEHOGS IN THE HALL	£3.50	☐
6	BADGER IN THE BASEMENT	£3.50	☐
7	CUB IN THE CUPBOARD	£3.50	☐
8	PIGLET IN A PLAYPEN	£3.50	☐
9	OWL IN THE OFFICE	£3.50	☐
10	LAMB IN THE LAUNDRY	£3.50	☑ 10
11	BUNNIES IN THE BATHROOM	£3.50	☐
12	DONKEY ON THE DOORSTEP	£3.50	☐
13	HAMSTER IN A HAMPER	£3.50	☐
14	GOOSE ON THE LOOSE	£3.50	☑ 14
15	CALF IN THE COTTAGE	£3.50	☐
16	KOALA IN A CRISIS	£3.50	☐
17	WOMBAT IN THE WILD	£3.50	☐
18	ROO ON THE ROCK	£3.50	☐
19	SQUIRRELS IN THE SCHOOL	£3.50	☑ 19
20	GUINEA-PIG IN THE GARAGE	£3.50	☐
21	FAWN IN THE FOREST	£3.50	☐
22	SHETLAND IN THE SHED	£3.50	☐
23	SWAN IN THE SWIM	£3.50	☐
24	LION BY THE LAKE	£3.50	☑ 24
25	ELEPHANTS IN THE EAST	£3.50	☐
26	MONKEYS ON THE MOUNTAIN	£3.50	☐
	SHEEPDOG IN THE SNOW	£3.50	☐
	KITTEN IN THE COLD	£3.50	☐
	SEAL ON THE SHORE	£3.50	☐
	FOX IN THE FROST	£3.50	☐